Paul
"I hope
your seeking
truth finds you!"
Ronald Raver

BOBBY AND TROUBDOUR'S GREAT ADVENTURE

In Search of the Dark Hole

A Journey of Self-Discovery

WRITTEN AND ILLUSTRATED BY
RONALD RAVER

Outskirts Press, Inc.
Denver, Colorado

Bobby and Troubadour's Great Adventure
In Search of the Dark Hole
All Rights Reserved.
Copyright © 2009 Ronald Raver.
V3.0 R1.0

Illustrations by Ronald Raver.

Outskirts Press, Inc.
http://www.outskirtspress.com

ISBN: 978-1-4327-2400-9

Library of Congress Number: 2009921790

Library of Congress Cataloging-in-Publication Data

Raver, Ronald, 1952—
    In search of the dark hole / Ronald Raver
        p. cm.—(Bobby and Troubadours great adventure ; 1)
        Summary: Bobby and other troubled teens embark on a treacherous journey with magical beings in search of an end to their personal pain, ultimately finding hope through God's love.
        [1. Suicide—Fiction. 2. Christian life—Fiction. 3. Self-discovery—Fiction. 4. Christian fantasy—Fiction. 5. Humorous stories] I. Title. II. Series: Raver, Ronald, 1952— . Bobby and Troubadour's great adventure ; #1.
        [Fic]

PRINTED IN THE UNITED STATES OF AMERICA

I dedicate this book to
my three grandchildren—Samantha, Erik, and Jessica
with the hope that they will always choose
to walk on the right paths.
And to my wife, Elizabeth, my constant encourager.

Acknowledgements

Special thanks to my daughter Andrea for all her support in typing and completing the first edit and to Lark Lamontagne for the final edit and putting it all together.

Foreword

As far back as I can remember, I battled with extreme boredom, chronic depression, and strong thoughts of suicide…even after I had become a Christian. One night after ministering to homeless people in Columbus, Ohio, I decided enough was enough and that I was going to put a stop to my never-ending pain once and for all.

All the way home on my fifty-minute drive, I could not escape the lies that the familiar voices in my head were always telling me—"you're not good enough…nobody really cares about you… everything is pointless… you're such a failure…," on and on the voices taunted. All my life I had felt that I never measured up to anyone's expectations, especially not my father's and certainly not God's, or so I wrongly believed.

As I pulled into my driveway and parked the car, my thoughts went to my unsuspecting family who lay sleeping upstairs …my wife and two kids who had no idea of what I was about to do. The voices continued, "they're better off without you...they'll get over it."

I got out of the car and walked down to the bridge that was within a rock's throw from my house. Emptiness engulfed me as I stared down into the swift, murky waters of the river below and I offered up one last half-hearted prayer to God before making ready to jump.

What happened next came as a total shock to me. I was no longer alone on the bridge—the Holy Spirit had joined me and he asked me, "Do you want to be free?"

"Yes!" was my heartfelt answer.

"Even if it costs you everything?" the Holy Spirit challenged.

Again, I earnestly answered Him with, "Yes!"

The next thing I knew, I was standing on the bridge alone once again.

For the next two years, everything I thought I knew about myself and about God was tested. During that time, all that I had worked so hard for in my life was stripped away. It was during those two years of struggle that this book was written.

Hidden in these pages is the truth I discovered about myself and the incredible process God used to bring restoration not only to my mind, but to my life as well. My hope in writing this book is that teens struggling with hurt and rejection will consider a different path other than wanting to end their life. Although the word "suicide" is never used in this book, suicide awareness and prevention is its underlying theme and is woven throughout its pages.

This story is about an undersized twelve-year-old named Bobby Cooper. After suffering an overwhelming disappointment, he sets out on an incredible journey in hopes of finding the Dark Hole, a place to bring his consuming pain to an end by surrendering his life.

Along the way, he crosses paths of four other teens with the same resolve, also searching for the Dark Hole. Their journey together becomes increasingly complicated when they encounter Damien, a sly, sinister snake and an enormous lovable creature named Troubadour.

Prologue

Have you ever been so desperate that you would do just about anything to ease your pain, knowing full well that your self-destructive actions would leave your family members and friends in an emotional train wreck? Never-the-less, you would press on with reckless abandon, pursuing anything that could stop the hurt.

Have you ever felt that any hope for happiness has long since passed you by, leaving you with just another dull day and a long dark night to deal with tormenting memories?

Has trying to live up to unrealistic expectations caused you to lose contact with yourself to the point that you don't even know who you are anymore and have lost your identity?

Although the word suicide isn't mentioned in this short story, its underlying theme is woven throughout its pages. The story deals with the emotional pain and mental anguish related to teen suicide. With each suicide there is a double tragedy, because along with the sudden loss resulting from a deliberated death, there are friends and family left with the question "why?"

Suicide attempts by teens can occur from something as simple (although painful) as a break up of a romance, school stresses, peer pressure, and goals that are thwarted…or the cause can be much more complicated such as dealing with rejection, permanent loneliness, chronic depression, pathological attitudes, or a disabling mental illness brought on by traumatic life events.

It may be hard to recognize the signs that a teen may be contemplating suicide because their sadness and hopelessness are often disguised as boredom, apathy, or physical restraints and complaints.

The disturbing rise in teen suicide in the United States over the last few years could be the result of increased alcoholism, drug use, breakdown of the family unit, child abuse, neglect or sexual assault.

This story will help you see how five teens deal with their journey leading to the Dark Hole, a place they believe will end their pain once and for all.

Contents

CHAPTER 1
A New Beginning

Still tired from a long night of tossing and turning, I finally managed to open one eye and then the other, slowly focusing on the radio alarm clock which was jarring me to my senses.

"Ughhhh…" I moaned as I laid there for a minute, motionless and still half asleep, staring at the ceiling fan that squeaked with every revolution. With one final stretch, I sat up and grabbed my glasses off the night stand, suddenly remembering why I went to bed fully dressed in play clothes the night before.

"Good morning, Summerset. It's going to be a gorgeous day today…There will be a pressure ridge settling over the Miami Valley region leaving us with plenty of sunshine and temperatures in the mid-eighties…zero percent chance of rain." The radio announcer's words were like music to my ears as he predicted the most perfect weather forecast ever.

"Even the gods are working in my favor today," I thought to myself. So with renewed strength and confidence, I leaned over and pushed the off button on my radio.

"Fantastic!" I shouted out loud as I tossed the bed sheet aside and jumped out of bed, looking around for the shoes I kicked off last night. Finding them lying across the room, I struggled to get them on without having to untie the shoestrings, hopping first on my left foot then the right while trying to keep my balance.

Not wasting any time, I made my way toward the bathroom sink, splashed some cold water on my face, and half-heartedly brushed my teeth. "Ooops…Mom won't like the mess I accidentally left on the mirror," I muttered.

I grabbed my lucky hat off the door hook and quickly pulled it onto my head, checking my hair out. I winked and pointed at the freckle-faced kid in the mirror saying, "You're the man!"

I raced down the hall and bounded down the stairs, taking two at a time, stumbling only once. I stopped in the kitchen just long enough to gobble down a chocolate Pop Tart, washing it down with a gulp of milk straight from the container. Quite to my surprise, I heard my mother's voice coming from the other side of the kitchen.

"Happy Birthday, Bobby!" There was a short pause and then, "You know better than that, son."

Wiping the milk dribble from my chin I responded, "Sorry, Mom, my bad." I proceeded to set the empty milk container on the counter, hoping to make a run for the door.

Before I knew it my mother came over and planted a big kiss on my forehead, asking if she could fix me some breakfast.

Frustrated by the hold up, I quickly responded, "No, Mom, you know I'm in a hurry… I really gotta go." I wondered why she couldn't see my rush.

She pointed toward her cheek for a return kiss and in a loving manner she said, "Alright, Bobby. I guess we'll have two things to celebrate when you return home tonight. You be careful and don't forget your helmet."

Irritated by the holdup and seeing my chance to escape, I quickly made my move toward the garage door blurting out, "Sure Mom, whatever."

Still thinking about how she just didn't get it, I retrieved my baseball equipment, glanced briefly at my helmet, and mounted my faithful steed—a ten-speed mountain bike. Then, I rode like the wind toward the Summerset Baseball Park located in the center of town. Even in all my haste as I pedaled down the street, I couldn't help but notice all the splendor of our small town.

The dew-covered grass was drying from the warmth of the morning sun as a light breeze gently danced through the tops of the tall maple trees lining the streets in front of our homes. Birds chirped out their early morning melodies as our sleepy little community was waking up to the busy schedule of a new day.

What a great day this was going to be... a tremendous day, no, a stupendous, colossal, glorious day! This was going to be MY day! This day could possibly be the most awesome day of my life, so far.

Pedaling through the intersection of Lincoln and Elm, I kept pushing myself to go faster, but the burning in my calf muscles screamed for me to slow down. I stopped once to retrieve my lucky hat which the wind had snatched from my head. The only other interruption between me and my destiny was an occasional horn blast from an angry driver. They couldn't even begin to understand how important this day was for me!

Now I bet you're wondering what the excitement is all about. What would make this day so special? Well, let me tell you. For years, the first Saturday of summer vacation meant the official opening of baseball season in Summerset, which dated back a hundred years or more. My father and his father before him played in the big game and both my older brothers played as well. Now it was my turn to take my place, to carry on the great heritage of the fine name of Cooper.

Finally arriving at the ball field, I was a bit winded and out of breath. I jumped off my bike while it was still rolling forward. It finally came to rest as a heaping pile in the tall grass, after bouncing off a nearby light pole rather abruptly. With one last sigh of relief, I grabbed my ball mitt from the bent handle bars of my bike and headed towards the Summerset Ball Field.

I guess at this time it might serve a purpose to introduce myself. My name is Bobby Thomas Cooper. I'm a scrappy 75-pound (soaking wet) twelve year-old honor student known to my friends as BC, the baseball-loving brainiac. Some other things you should know about me—I am shy, but highly motivated... uncoordinated, but very intellectual... I could go on, but I don't want to bore you. Let's get back to the big game.

As special as this day was to be for me, it wasn't without its risks. The important thing to understand is that this opportunity comes only once in your life, in your twelfth year. Every twelve-year old in Summerset is eligible to participate in the big game and it was my twelfth birthday today.

As I took my place with the other twelve year-olds, little beads of sweat began to form on my forehead. With my glove and bat in tow, I found a place in line by the fence that surrounded the field of battle, better known as the Summerset Baseball Field. There we stood like a squad of highly-trained soldiers, standing at attention during inspection, with all the weapons needed to accomplish the task at hand.

I was feeling even more secure than before because of the light turn-out of participants. I calmly reassured myself by occasionally taking a couple of deep breaths and trying to enjoy the festive atmosphere by watching the bleachers fill to capacity with enthusiastic supporters.

Minutes seemed like hours and I began to realize the arches in my feet had begun to ache. This was because I was standing on my toes to appear taller than I was, hoping to gain any advantage I could over the other combatants assembled there today. Intense fear began to ease its way into my racing heart. Yet, in spite of all my efforts to control my composure, it began. First one drop, then two, and then what felt like hundreds of sweat beads began to run down my back as if they were having a race to form a puddle in the small of my back.

Not to lose my focus on the things at hand, I pulled my shirttail out of the top of my black shorts to get a little air flow to the wet spot and I then shifted my attention onto the tantalizing smells of hotdogs and popcorn.

There was an eerie silence, like the calm before the storm as I noticed my pulse quickening and those beads of sweat have turned into full blown perspiration. I think, "Why didn't I put on any deodorant today?" I knew what was about to take place would bring fear to the bravest of kid's hearts, that dreaded process of elimination, otherwise known as the captain's choosing up sides.

The more talented kids hold your destiny in the palm of their hands, or at least the end of their pointing finger. The nightmare begins with the first choice of players, "I choose Zack, I'll take Gary..."

Two more names were called as I realize my confident smile was quickly turning into a sheepish grin. Two more names called, one by one, on my right and on my left. But there I stood... resembling some type of stone statue, motionless and unable to move a muscle, paralyzed by mounting humiliation.

Nervously, I lost focus as my thoughts wandered back to last summer when my family was vacationing in the Smokey Mountains. There we were cruising down the highway with our top down, enjoying the fresh air as it blew through our hair. Suddenly, a deer darted onto the highway directly in front of my father's new convertible. The weirdest thing was that deer froze in its tracks blinded by our headlights...right in the middle of the road, braced for impact. This made absolutely no sense to me because all the reckless creature needed to do was continue on its way across the road.

But yet, there I stood, frozen in the headlights of life, fixed in time, glued to the earth, unable to take a step in any direction. I offered up a quick, half-hearted prayer to the man upstairs, "Please let them choose me!" Then those dreaded mind games begin, like: What on earth was I thinking when I picked out this shirt? Wondering if my shorts match, or not...

Two more names were called, with high fives everywhere, and cheers of joy. Two more of the athletes join in the victor's huddle. I began to feel that gnawing, empty feeling that hits you right in the pit of your stomach. I decided to practice my breathing techniques...breath in with the good, and breathe out with the bad. Hope returns momentarily as I realized the more talented and popular kids have already been chosen.

The normal and average kids are left but before I know it, my confidence turns to fear, and fear to panic as I reach for the brown paper sack I put in my back pocket just in case I hyperventilate again. My self-esteem begins to act like a butterfly, softly fluttering in the summer breeze, as it dances from flower to flower until it disappears into the distance.

Now my glasses were beginning to steam up due to my sweat glands turning on me. I used the sleeve of my shirt to dry the perspiration from the lens of my glasses, and my thoughts decided to skip off to do their own thing again, stopping to rest on my last book assignment at school about the astronauts of Apollo 13.

Now I was able to better understand what they must have felt when they found themselves in that hopeless situation in space... but I was more perturbed than ever, thinking that even in the midst of their ruin, the astronauts at least had the Houston Command Center to contact for support. I had absolutely no one to console me.

I found myself clapping every so often in agreement as if to pretend I cared, telling myself, "Bobby, don't go there." Now a new dilemma arose...I needed to go to the restroom.

I glance down the fence line to notice only three candidates are left, including myself. On my right was Arnold-the chubby kid, who is eating every time you saw him...and on my left is Casey-the biggest tomboy in the whole, wide world.

I stood there with the worst possible scenario unfolding right before my eyes. I didn't even hear the next two selections...all I know is Arnold ran to one group of screaming kids and Casey was jumping for joy as she ran to the other group of kids. I knew at that moment, every eye was fixed on me like little lasers...and the only thing I could think to do was run.

I dropped my bat and glove and started running as fast as my feet would carry me. I ran and ran until I thought my heart was going to beat right out of my chest. Stopping only once to water a nearby tree, I ran and ran until I couldn't take another step. Totally exhausted, I fell to the ground.

I thought to myself, "How could this happen to me on this, my special day!" I pounded the ground with my fist as tears streamed down my cheeks. I cried out, "I can't believe I got beat out by a girl. Sure she could run faster, jump higher and catch better than me...but she still is only a girl! It's not fair!"

Regaining strength fueled by my anger, I got back up and started to run again. I continued to run with reckless abandon, darting between trees and jumping over limbs that cluttered the ground. Soon nothing looked familiar... I had actually run far deeper into the woods than I had ever gone before.

There was a chill in the air that sent a shiver up my spine. Feeling weak in the knees, I collapsed into the damp weeds at the base of an old willow tree, wondering what to do next. Suddenly the looming shadows began to engulf me, blocking out what was left of the sun's light and warmth. I began to shake, thinking, "I sure wish I had my jacket."

As I sat there shivering from the cold, something really weird happened, something I still have a hard time believing. It started as a low hissing whisper and soon turned into an audible voice. I looked up to find its source, and to my amazement, looking back at me was this enormous snake wearing black sunglasses...and he was grinning at me.

The snake laughingly said, "Hey, squirt, what's up? Yeah you, girly-boy. Kind of small and bony, aren't you?"

I sat there shaking my head in disbelief, pretending not to hear a word he was saying.

Smiling from ear-to-ear the snake taunted, "I know you can hear me, kid, so stop pretending you can't. You look really stupid and we both know you don't need any help to do that."

Still exhausted from my long run through the woods and now becoming more than a little irritated with the snake, I blurted out, "Why don't you just shut up?"

"Make me, if you think you can, shrimp," challenged, the reptile while angrily hissing at me. This multi-colored monster of a snake had to be at least thirty feet long and I doubted that I could make him do anything, period.

Uncoiling his long, muscular body from around the outstretched tree limb, the talkative reptile changed positions. Casually leaning back against the trunk of the old willow tree, he gingerly wiped his forehead with his long slender tail, "I know your day hasn't turned out the way you hoped, but that doesn't give you the right to be rude or take out your disappointment on me, kid"

Repositioning himself back up onto the limb, the snake continued to ramble on…"I mean all I'm trying to do, kid, is understand what you might be feeling since I've never failed at anything that I've tried…" The snotty snake continued, "Actually, I'm just trying to be helpful, my bony little friend. And we both know you could use all the help you can get, don't we?" The old-smart-mouthed snake snickered and flashed another toothy grin.

Taking his attention off of me momentarily, my so-called friend suddenly lunged without provocation in the direction of an unsuspecting field mouse and swallowed it whole. Before I could open my mouth, the snake was wiping his lips with the end of his tail and his enormous body was back resting on the tree limb once again.

"That's really sick..." I shook my head and looked away as he let out this really loud, nasty burp.

"Wha-a-a-at? You got to eat, don't you?" Picking at his fang with a twig from a tree branch, the shameless snake smiled and jokingly said, "Do you want me to get you one?"

"No thanks!" I snapped. Confused and fed up with the snake's mouth, I added, "I just want to be left alone right now…so why don't you just mind your own business?" I slumped down as another hunger pang gnawed at my stomach.

Hissing on every sentence the snake mockingly said, "Well shorty, I've made you my business, haven't I? I'm curious…what were you, the runt of the litter?"

Stinging from his last insult, I said, "Excuse me, snakes can't talk." Looking down momentarily, hoping when I look back up my nightmare will be over and that lippy, good-for-nothing reptile will be gone.

But to my surprise when I looked up again, the snake was smiling and waving at me with his tail as if to say, "I'm still here."

Shaking my head to clear it, more confused than ever, I mumbled, "Oh great, he's still here!" Then, smacking myself on both sides of my head repeatedly, I yelled, "You don't exist! You just don't exist! You are only a figment of my imagination!"

"Can your imagination do this?" His tail swiftly flicked my left ear, knocking my hat off in the process.

"O-O-U-C-H!," I yelled, "What is up with that?" I demanded as I rubbed my throbbing ear.

"Just trying to get your attention, squirt," laughed the snake. He uncoiled himself to get a closer look at me. He said, "Let me take this opportunity to introduce myself." His hand-like tail removed his sunglasses revealing two of the biggest, dark green eyes that stuck out like two glittering emeralds. "I go by the name of Damien, but you can call me anything you would like since I really don't exist except in your imagination...or do I? Now that we've been officially introduced, I can't help but notice how sad you are, and that deeply hurts me, too!" He put his glasses back on and said, "It saddens me greatly to see you in this condition. I have the solution to your problem, to stop your pain."

The snake uncoiled his long body just enough to slip his tail around my shoulders giving me an insincere hug, but I fell for it. Wiping my eyes, I said, "Damien, it hurts so much. Kids can be so heartless, can't they?"

"I know, Bobby," crooned Damien, pretending that he cared. "But what if I could show you a place where you would never be hurt or rejected ever again...where kids would never be mean to you again. Would you be interested?"

"Is it far?" I said reluctantly.

9

Damien said, "Bobby, it won't take you long at all, because you're already half way there and don't even realize it. Just keep on following that trail."

As quickly as he appeared, Damien disappeared into the branches of the old willow tree, saying, "See you around, kid." Then he added, "Oh, by the way, Happy Birthday, squirt."

Sitting back against the trunk of the tree I wondered to myself how the snake had known it was my birthday. The sun gave way to the moon. I was tired, hungry, and cold. I begin to reflect about the conversation I just had with Damien. If only it would be possible to go to a place where you would never have to experience the pain of rejection again. I rested my head upon my knees and prepared for a very dark, scary night. A barn owl serenaded me with a lullaby as I fell off to sleep.

CHAPTER 2
A New Friend

With my clothing damp and mildewed from the early morning dew, I awoke to the forest's crisp, clear air and its symphony of sounds surrounding me. The owl that had serenaded me to sleep the night before was now replaced by a family of woodpeckers tapping out a secret code in perfect rhythm.

Cold and confused, filled with nothing but uncertainty, there I sat… Still unable to totally understand the series of events that I lived through yesterday, especially my conversation with Damien, the snake.

As hard as it was to believe that I talked to a snake, my human consciousness was not prepared to grasp what I saw next. Sitting there in disbelief, I pinched myself to make sure I wasn't still asleep.

There beside me was the biggest pile of fruit consisting of apples, grapes, and pears—all sliced to perfection. Over to my left, lying in a hammock tied between two large oak trees, was an astonishing creature singing a little jingle, "Walking in love, walking in the light, every morning, noon and night."

Famished, I sat there in stunned silence gobbling up most of the fruit assortment. Finally full, I stood up and cautiously approached the hammock, making sure to keep a safe distance between me and the enormous creature. "Excuse me…who are you and better yet, what are you?" I still couldn't believe my eyes.

Sitting straight up in the hammock with a warm smile the creature said, "My friends call me Troubadour, and for what I am, it shouldn't matter." Jumping down from the hammock while straightening his wrinkled clothes, he stuck out a big paw for me to shake, "And your name is?"

"Bobby. Bobby Cooper," I couldn't help but stare at him for he stood at least eight feet tall, from head to toe. His body mostly resembled a lion but he walked upright like a man. Everything about him said he was extremely strong. Each step he took pointed to the fact that he was confident in whom he was and everything about him demanded respect.

Fixing both of his large paws securely under my armpits, the gentle giant hoisted my whole body off the ground, leaving my feet dangling beneath me. It was as though I had been connected to this enormous construction crane and now was being lifted into the sky.

I felt so inadequate, compared to the sheer physical size of Troubadour, which defied description. There I was, now eye to eye with this kindly, furry creature. His deep, dark brown eyes sparkled brilliantly like my mother's fine crystal.

With my feet still dangling and my eyes tightly closed, I took a deep breath and blurted out, "Are you going to eat me?" I hoped he would be sympathetic.

To my extreme astonishment when I opened my eyes, my feet were now firmly planted on the ground and to my amazement the big, loveable creature was doubled up with laughter. Stopping only long enough to jokingly spit out, "You've got to be kidding, kid... you don't have enough meat on your bones for a good snack."

Troubadour grabbed his stomach from laughing so hard and said, "Besides that...you would probably give me gas." Then he proceeded to put his forearm to his mouth, blowing against it to produce a farting sound, with that he laughed even harder.

15

Feeling my temper rise from being laughed at, I picked up a couple sticks from the forest floor and threw them at Troubadour who was now rolling around in the dirt, consumed with laughter.

Then I yelled, "Get up! You look ridiculous. You're an embarrassment to yourself as well as me!" Throwing my hands in the air and mumbling, "And people say I have unresolved issues…"

Trying to regain composure, Troubadour rose to his feet while holding his sides from laughing so hard. He then walked over to a fallen maple tree where he sat down. Patting the tree trunk with his paw, he beckoned me to join him.

Reluctantly, I took a seat next to Troubadour, and much to my surprise I unceremoniously started telling him all my troubles as soon as my rump hit that log. I described in detail my living nightmare of not being picked by either team for the big game, communicating the whole humiliating story that brought me so much hurt. Hoping for a little sympathy I ended my story with, "Well, that's how I got here, Troubadour."

While nibbling on a few slugs he had pulled off the log's bark, Troubadour looked in my direction and calmly responded, "Sometimes we work so hard at being something we are not, that we totally miss out on the thing we were created to be."

Feeling my temper rise again, I jumped to my feet and shouted, "That's it! That's all I get? Some philosophical mumbo jumbo?"

While Troubadour dug into the bark of the fallen tree, the soft-spoken beast questioned, "What did you expect, a pity-party?"

Here I sat, just like Mount Saint Helen's in Washington State. My temper was boiling and becoming increasingly hotter by the second. I stewed in all my insecurities, waiting for that perfect moment to erupt in rage, spewing magma on anyone foolish enough to be in my way.

Seeing my opening, I jumped to my feet with all the intensity of an erupting volcano and yelled, "Pity-party….pity-party? Did I hear you correctly…Did you say pity-party?" I was thinking even that cold-blooded reptile Damien showed more compassion and sensitivity than Troubadour had.

After a couple more minutes of ranting and raving, I got myself under control by taking a couple deep breaths. I hurled a stone that I had picked up into the tree tops, watching birds scatter from their secure perches.

Weary from pacing, stomping, and kicking everything that came in range of my temper tantrum, I gave one last desperate cry for help. "Is anyone out there? Does anyone care?" My voice trailed off as I realized that my hands were full of my own hair.

With my head down in embarrassment, I started to walk over to where Troubadour was still patiently sitting. I removed my glasses and wiped the sweat from my forehead.

"I'm sorry, big guy...I don't know what comes over me sometimes."

Troubadour nodded to say he understood and then responded, "You're kind of a scrappy little fellow aren't you, Bobby?

Troubadour fished a toothpick out of his pocket and started digging at some bug's remains that had gotten lodged in his rather large, pearly whites. After dusting some termite wings from the lap of his blue denim coveralls, he rose to his feet tossing the used toothpick to the ground, commenting "That was a nice snack."

Then he walked over to me and compassionately put his enormous paw on my shoulder. "Bobby, life is like a good book. It's most important parts are where it begins and how it ends. All the other pages of the book will change at the discretion of the author's pen."

"If I understand you correctly, Troubadour, life is nothing more than a series of choices. The consequences of your choices are what determine which direction that your life will go."

"Exactly, Bobby, so make good choices."

I figuratively patted myself on the back boasting, "That's why I'm the smartest kid in my middle school class."

Thinking back to what Damien shared with me yesterday, I asked Troubadour if he knew of a place called the Dark Hole. And if he did, would he help me find it?

Straightening the red braids of his long, wild chin-hairs (which reminded me of my uncle's goatee), Troubadour answered, "I certainly do, but it's in the opposite direction of where we need to go! Besides, your parents must be very worried by now."

"I doubt it."

Troubadour responded, "Are you sure of that?"

"Yes especially not my dad. I've never been able to live up to that man's expectations. Once, after a sporting event in which I let him down, I heard my father telling my older brother that he finally got the little girl he'd always wanted. That really hurt me, Troubadour."

Troubadour slid his large arm around my neck and said, "I'm so sorry, Bobby."

Pulling away so he couldn't see my tears, I replied, "Don't be...I just don't fit in anywhere. Will you help me find the Dark Hole, or not?" I said trying to act tough.

Troubadour pointed to the trail and said, "Well, are you ready to start your journey? Everything you will need has already been provided for you."

CHAPTER 3
A New Way of Thinking

The two of us had been walking for a couple of hours, enjoying the wonderful scent of the lilac trees which lined the narrow path we were on. Occasionally, a sunbeam would penetrate the heavy density of the tall trees, illuminating the trail and drying up the last of the morning dew. As we walked Troubadour and I had a great conversation—we talked about school, friends and family matters. Then we started on my favorite topic, books.

Troubadour asked, "So Bobby, do you like to read?"

I replied, "I'd rather read than just about anything except playing or watching baseball."

Digging in his coveralls for a comb he asked, "Do you have a favorite book?"

While watching a couple of rabbits hop across the path I answered Troubadour's question, "Superman Returns."

"Why?" asked Troubadour. As he spoke a beautiful, multi-colored Monarch butterfly flew over and sat peaceably on Troubadour's long, reddish brown hair.

Eagerly I explained, "Superman gets beat down by the villains, abandoned by his girlfriend, and insulted by the very people he had helped. Even though he feels really dejected from all of this, he never loses sight of his driving purpose!" I shook my head in amazement and continued "In his weakened state, superman flies directly into the path of the sun…"

"Flies?" interrupted Troubadour.

"Well yeah…everyone knows the Man of Steel flies… duh!" Wondering what planet this creature came from, I asked him, "Do they have books where you come from? Can you read?"

"I read very well, if you please!" Troubadour said with a smile. "But unlike you humans who read for enjoyment and the love of a good book, my created species reads for enlightenment. We read to achieve knowledge that would aid us in accomplishing the destiny we were created for."

"Bor…ring!" I said laughing as Troubadour captured me in a playful headlock.

After wiggling out of Troubadour's vice grip and picking up my hat off the ground I said, "Just kidding, big guy." Then I asked if he had a certain book he preferred to read as well.

"Sure do…it comes from my favorite book, the Book of Life." Troubadour started to share this incredible story. "The book speaks of a most exalted King that is worshipped and highly praised, who was righteous in all his ways. His kingdom was not built by hands but spoken into existence by the Word. His kingdom, set high on a hill, is a city of emeralds, rubies, and jasper seas. It was held in place by the breath of the Creator, fueled by the passion of his eternal flames."

Next thing I know, and much to my surprise, Troubadour bent his head in mid-sentence, fell upon both his knees, and continued to say, "This almighty King, made these magnificent creatures for his enjoyment, these angelic beings. Then he named them, one by one; Gabriel, Michael, and Lucifer. All of them helped the King to rule and reign over the kingdom."

Troubadour's voice began to turn angry, "Then Lucifer, son of the Morning Star, said in his heart that it's not enough, I want to be King. I will ascend into the heaven. I will exalt my throne above the stars of the King. I will ascend above the heights of the clouds. I will be like the King, Most High."

"Because of this, there was a war in the glorious kingdom. Michael and his angels stood on the high ground, Lucifer and the fallen angels on the lower ground. And the Book of Life said

Lucifer and his angels had no chance of winning and were cast out."

Interrupting Troubadour, I said, "Cool story…do you know if it's been released in DVD yet?"

Without warning or hesitation, that enormous creature rose to his feet in a defensive posture that reminded me of a periscope on a submarine rising out of the ocean searching for trouble. Every hair in his thick, wavy mane was standing to attention readied for battle.

It was the first time I felt real danger being in the presence of this gentle giant. Timidly, I asked, "Everything alright?"

I received no response from him. He just stood there motionless, staring into the thick grove of trees immediately in front of us, taking on the appearance of a furious lion ready to attack.

Not knowing what to do next, I decided to take a karate stance I saw in a movie last week, thinking that whatever is out there, it's about to get a butt whooping…if I don't wet my pants first.

I can't begin to explain, let alone understand what happened next. All I know is this green blur shot past me like a guided missile finding its target nose-to-nose with Troubadour. There they stood, like two gang members ready to fight each other.

With the dust settling, I said, "Good Morning, Damien."

Never taking his emerald eyes off of Troubadour, Damien angrily replied, "Morning, kid."

The showdown continued with both creatures circling each other like a couple of caged animals.

More dishonorable than ever, Damien said with a sinister hiss, "He's mine, fur ball. It's what the boy has chosen!"

With Troubadour's forehead pressed up firmly against Damien's forehead, he roared, "I'm not here to change the course of the boy… I've been sent to shine some light on his path."

Stepping in between the two combatants, I screamed, "Alright already! Would someone please tell me what's going on here?" I was tired of being left out.

21

Without my permission, Troubadour gently shuttled me behind his back with his rather muscular arm. Then turning his attention back to the snake said, "Damien, we'll be on our way now."

Damien hissed, "This isn't over yet, Troubadour." With Damien's dark green eyes fixed solely on me, he jeered, "For once in your life, Bobby, make your father proud and see something through to the end." Slithering off into the tall grass, he looked back at us flashing a nasty smile.

CHAPTER 4
Two for the Price of One

Troubadour and I silently started down the path again. After walking for what seemed like hours, the path ended momentarily. We came upon this most wonderful little clearing, like a picture perfect moment that you very seldom have the privilege of experiencing.

There were thousands and thousands of fluttering butterflies skirting about the tops of these beautiful flowers of many colors. The flowers danced to a gentle breeze as if they were performing a musical for our enjoyment. Much to my surprise, right in the midst of all this beauty were two kids that stuck out like a couple of sore thumbs.

The boy was dressed from head to toe in black clothing, with chains dangling everywhere. A younger girl was kneeling at his side holding tightly to his waist as if she was glued to him, sobbing rather hard.

Troubadour and I got a little closer to them and I saw the older boy stroking the hair of the young girl trying to reassuring her. "Don't worry… in a little while, it isn't going to hurt anymore."

We approached the two of them very slowly so as not to startle them. I said, "Hello, my name is Bobby," I stuck my hand out to shake hands and continued, "and this big guy here goes by the name of Troubadour. What are your names?"

The boy in black said "I'll be your worst nightmare if you don't leave us alone." Then he proceeded to poke me hard in the chest with his finger.

I grabbed his wrist and held his arm as he struggled to pull it away. "What's up with that? We're just trying to be your friend."

"What makes you think I need any friends?"

Troubadour then took one of those big fingers of his and gently touched the tip of the little girl's nose.

"Hey you, freak! Leave her alone! She doesn't like to be touched." Then the young girl buried her face deeper into the boy's chest, only peeking out momentarily to see if we had left yet.

What Troubadour did next amazed even me.

He said, "So what brings you and Cindy out here, Billy? Why aren't you home with your mother? She must be worried."

Shielding her eyes from the bright sun, Cindy mumbled. "How do you know our names?"

Billy put his finger in Troubadour's face and said, "You may know our names, but you know nothing about us, so why don't you mind your own business…You got it?" He removed his finger from Troubadour's face and sneered at me.

Removing my glasses to appear meaner than I was, I snapped back, "Why don't you lighten up already, we were just trying to help."

Crazed with anger, Billy rushed at me like a bull in an open pasture. Thank goodness for my sake, Troubadour interfered by stepping in the way.

"Help me? Are you kidding? No one else would help us."

Billy's face contorted and he began to fight back tears. "All right," he gasped, "if you're so smart, then tell me why our parents had to split up. Why they couldn't love Cindy and me enough to work out their differences…Why my mother did absolutely nothing to stop our stepfather from hurting Cindy, usually at night when everyone else was asleep?"

Cindy's frail body still heaving, pleaded, "Why didn't my mother believe me, her own daughter! I guess she loves that man more than she loves me! I feel so dirty, so ugly..." She buried her face in her hands sobbing, unable to stop.

At that point, I think I even saw a tear fall from Troubadour's eye. He stood there listening with his face full of compassion as he watched Billy wrap his arms around his little sister.

"No one would believe us or stop him so Cindy and I ran away from home last night. We ended up here, where you found us today. Last night we crossed paths with a snake named Damien who told us about a place that he knows of, a place where no one could hurt my sister again. It's a place where we can end the pain once and for all. Damien called the place The Dark Hole."

"Call me insensitive or just plain stupid, but I don't understand why your sister is so upset. How exactly did your stepdad hurt Cindy?"

Troubadour quickly reached over and put his big paw on my shoulder. "Some things are better not talked about, okay?"

Before I knew it, Billy got up in my face "Why don't you mind your own business, punk?" jamming his finger in my chest again.

It really ticked me off this time.

With the same amount of force, I crammed my finger into Billy's chest, yelling, "At least I don't look like some medieval, gothic pin cushion!" I thought to myself that all those piercings must have hurt, especially the one through his tongue.

Seeing the tension, Troubadour stepped between us and said, "Gentlemen, we have a long journey ahead of us, so can we please learn to play nicely together?"

"Yeah, sure," muttered Billy.

I whispered to Billy, "I bet your report cards say you don't play well with other children."

Billy put his sister up on his shoulders to give her a well-needed rest as they began to walk. Then he whispered so that Troubadour couldn't hear him, "Yeah, well you're still a four-eyed punk! And ugly to boot."

CHAPTER 5
A Common Cause

We all started down the path to the Dark Hole with Billy and I still whispering insults to each other while Troubadour sang that little jingle to himself, just loud enough for us to hear. It was the same one he was singing when I first met him: "Walking in love, walking in the light, every morning, noon, and night."

As we walked quietly down the narrow, tree-lined path, I couldn't help but think to myself how insignificant the pain I felt was compared to the pain Cindy and her brother were suffering. Not being picked to play in a baseball game wasn't anything like what they were dealing with.

I followed the two of them, watching them interact together. I began to realize that even though we were bound together by the common thread of pain and rejection, the three of us were still very much alone in dealing with our own despair.

It seemed as though we had walked for days, but in reality, it had been only a few hours. The sun was working overtime, baking us like turkeys in an oven. It's funny what your mind can do—thinking about baking turkey had made me realize how hungry I was. Unfortunately for us the only creatures enjoying a meal were some nasty, blood-sucking mosquitoes as they took turns feasting on us. It's a wonder we all didn't get malaria or something.

Troubadour said, "Look up there," pointing to three buzzards crisscrossing in the sky, alerting us to a problem.

Suddenly, the normal quiet of the forest was interrupted by a faint cry off in the distance. We tried hard to listen and figure out where the S.O.S. calls were coming from.

We headed towards the circling buzzards—stopping just long enough to help Cindy up after she stumbled over a tree limb that had fallen across the path. We reached a small hill and started climbing to the top of what seemed like Mount Everest.

Once we reached the top, we looked down into the valley below. Much to our surprise we saw a boy and a wheelchair lying there in a crumpled pile, covered in dirt. The boy was desperately trying to straighten out his crippled legs and get into a sitting position. Every so often, he would cry out for help.

While Billy and I looked at each other wondering what we could do to rescue him, Troubadour had already put a plan into action. He was tugging with all his might at some vines hanging off a nearby Sequoia tree. With sweat dripping off of Troubadour's brow, he managed to detach five long vines from their roots.

Wasting no time, Billy and I ran to tie the ends together. Unfortunately, we both ran to the same vine and started our own tug of war contest, while Cindy cheered her brother on. I believe I was holding my own until Troubadour got involved by yanking the middle of the vine we were fighting over. It immediately sent Billy and I sprawling forward, face first into the dirt.

Troubadour roared with disapproval, "We have better ways of spending our time than to waste another minute on your petty disagreements!" He pointed to the vines lying on the ground and said, "Would you two please help me by tying their ends together?"

I went one way and Billy went the other, glaring at each other as we went. We knelt down to tie all the vine ends together and then lowered the vine rope down to the ravine floor while Troubadour secured one end to a large boulder stationed at the top of the ravine.

Reaching down with one of his big paws, Troubadour snatched Cindy up, lifting her straight up onto his back. "Hang on, sweetie," he said. Following his command Cindy hung on, firmly attached to Troubadour's back like a tick on a hound dog. Troubadour carefully stepped over the edge of the cliff and methodically climbed down into the ravine.

Billy and I looked at each other, and without a word raced to the rock to see who would be next. Once we had all made it to the bottom of the ravine, Troubadour picked up the wheelchair and set it upright. Billy and I got under each of the boy's arms and helped him back into his wheelchair. Cindy handed him his gloves.

The boy fought hard not to cry as his eyes filled with tears. He yelled, "I hate myself and these stupid, good for nothing legs of mine!" He proceeded to hit his legs with his fists. "I'm useless and can't do anything...I hate my life!" sobbed the boy.

Billy said, "Well if you really hate your life as much as you say you do, why don't you consider coming with us. We all hate our miserable lives, too!"

Then Troubadour spoke up, "Excuse me! I enjoy life to the fullest, if you please! I've learned to be content with whatever the day brings my way."

Billy said, "If life were only that simple, right Cindy?" Cindy's only response was to squeeze her brother's hand a bit tighter.

While making little quotation marks with my fingers, I mockingly chimed in with "If only."

Reaching into the front pouch of his coveralls, Troubadour pulled out a bright red bandana and said, "You'll need this."

Cindy looked away as her brother said, "Yeah, the back of your head is bleeding pretty bad, dude!"

Wiping the remaining tears from his cheeks and taking the bandana from Troubadour, the boy in the wheelchair said, "Thanks... If it wasn't for bad luck, I'd have no luck at all!"

Applying pressure to the wound on the back of his head he continued, "I have absolutely no feeling below my waist and now I end up with a head injury...and a headache."

Smiling, I said, "Your luck is about to change. Why don't you come with us in search of the Dark Hole?"

"So dude, what do you think...Want to join us?" Billy coaxed.

The boy in the wheelchair said, "What is the Dark Hole?"

Billy continued by saying, "It's a place where you will never be hurt or need to live up to anyone's expectations again!"

The boy asked, "Do you know if that place really exists?"

Billy replied, "A snake named Damien told us about it."

The boy shook his head yes and said, "It's probably the same snake that pushed my wheelchair off that cliff."

"Well," I said, "since it sounds like you'll be joining us, I guess I'll do the introductions. I'm Bobby; this big guy to my left is Troubadour."

The boy checked out Troubadour from head to toe.

"The kid in black goes by the name of Billy and this is Cindy, his little sister." Billy pulled Cindy out from behind him.

Raising his hand in a salute, the boy in the wheelchair said, "Charlie Campbell at your service." He smiled gratefully and added, "I really appreciate the help, you guys."

Desperately wanting to put an end to our pain once and for all, we set off in search of the Dark Hole. We had been walking for awhile when we started to notice that the path was disappearing due to an undergrowth of thick brush. Stickers and bramble bushes on each side of the path were attacking our arms and legs with our every step, leaving scratches and cuts on us everywhere.

This made the mosquitoes even more aggressive. The path got so narrow at times we ended up going single file on our hands and knees. As difficult as that was for us, imagine the difficulty poor Charlie was having with his wheelchair. We had to stop often to get sticks and brush out of the spokes of his wheels.

It was taking a tremendous amount of time to gain even little advances on this part of the trail. Our clothing was ripped and torn, shredded from the thorns and thistles. Dirty and bloody, we kept pressing on knowing that the momentary hardships we were facing would soon be over. I remembered what my dad once told me. If it doesn't kill you, it surely will make you stronger.

Then out of nowhere, we came upon another clearing. In the middle of the clearing was a giant apple tree with its branches full of the biggest, reddest, and juiciest-looking apples that I'd ever seen—just inviting us to come eat.

We approached the tree slowly thinking it might only be a mirage tricking our senses. Once we realized the apple tree was real, we began to eat our fill of those delicious apples and stuffed some more into our pockets for later. We sat under the apple tree enjoying the shade and much needed rest, reluctant to leave.

After straightening my legs out to relax in the tall, soft grass and using the wheel of Charlie's chair for my head rest, I was now prepared for a nice, late afternoon nap. But before I could fall off to sleep, I blurted out without thinking, "So Charlie, how'd you end up in the wheelchair?"

By the uncomfortable silence combined with the look on Troubadour's face, it probably wasn't the brightest thing I've ever done...Just call me, Mr. Insensitive.

With this awful blank stare on his face, Charlie started to share with us the tragic events leading up to his nightmare. Choking back tears Charlie said, "It was a beautiful Friday afternoon and we had just won the most important soccer match in my school's history, the middle school soccer championship. I scored the three goals that won us the game. I remember I was so happy I could barely contain myself...Shoot, my girlfriend gave me a kiss right in the middle of the field right after the game ended. Can you imagine what it feels like running off the field to a crowd yelling your name in unison? Charlie....Charlie....Charlie!"

Throwing my half-eaten apple at the trunk of the apple tree we were sitting under, I said, "I really can't say that I do." I adjusted my glasses and said, "You still haven't said how you lost the use of your legs, dude."

Charlie reached in his front pocket and took a couple blasts from an inhaler. He returned it to his pocket as he tried to catch his breath. Billy leaned over and said, "Smart move, dork. I bet you pull wings off of flies, too."

I snapped back, "Why don't you mind your own business?"

Cindy, normally quiet, chose that moment to speak up and defend her brother, "Funny, I was just thinking the same thing about you!"

I looked at Troubadour with my hands held out innocently and asked, "Wha-a-at?"

The gentle giant got up from where he was lounging and walked over to Charlie putting those big, loving arms around his shoulders. He smiled as he said, "You don't have to talk about it if you don't want to, Charlie."

Tears streaming down his cheeks, Charlie's said, "That's okay, Troubadour. It is what it is."

Just as I was getting ready to apologize, Charlie continued, "There I was, on top of my game. I had a pretty girlfriend, popularity, and a great future ahead of me. Then...from out of nowhere, this stupid drunk driver plowed into me while I was walking home. He sped off leaving my crushed body for dead with these two useless pieces of crap." He motioned at his legs. "When I woke up in the hospital my parents were crying since my doctor had told them that I'd never walk again. It wasn't too long after that my girlfriend broke up with me because she couldn't handle going out with a cripple. I can't blame her... I'm totally useless now."

Troubadour softly said, "You're not useless, Charlie. There's a lot you can do...You might consider coaching kids' soccer. I'm sure you would be great at it."

Ignoring Troubadour, Charlie lowered his head into his hands and said, "The only option I have left is to find that place called the Dark Hole and fall in."

Troubadour sat down and leaned against the old apple tree. Cindy lay with her red head cushioned in her brother's lap as she traced his arm tattoos with her finger. I just sat there watching all those tall trees swaying in the wind, thinking to myself how sad it was that Charlie couldn't see any better option than the Dark Hole.

CHAPTER 6
Shattered Perfection

The five of us still relaxing, watched the beginning of a sunset silhouetted by the tree-lined horizon. We couldn't help but notice the brilliant colors that streaked across the sky, allowing for a perfect moment in time—so peaceful and tranquil.

Then, abruptly, our almost therapeutic event was interrupted. Out of nowhere, a streak of lighting in the form of a girl blew by us like a gazelle with a hungry lion on her tail. She yelled without looking back at us, "You had better run!"

We looked at each other in amazement wondering what on earth that was all about. Soon, we got the answer to our question when Billy pointed to the sky and yelled, "RUN!" A swarm of very angry hornets were headed right for us.

We immediately took off running. The apples we had just collected were being tossed everywhere. In our panic to get to safety, we forgot poor old Charlie sitting in his wheelchair.

When we returned to where we left him, it was definitely not a pretty sight. Fortunately for Charlie, he's not allergic to bee stings.

Troubadour was already beginning to apply some juice from a plant he had collected earlier that day. Of course, I wondered how Troubadour knew we would need that for first aid. "Kind of spooky," I thought.

As soon as Troubadour was finished, we were on our way again. It wasn't long before we caught sight of our lightning bolt…Gosh, she was pretty!

There was the girl of my dreams sitting on a rock surrounded by a spectacular assortment of brilliantly colored flowers. As we got closer to the girl, I could tell the other flowers lost some of their luster in the presence of the prettiest orchid in the bunch. (Wow, I was beginning to think like some of those weird poets we studied in English class…Scary!)

Her long golden blonde hair was glistening in the sunlight as a gentle breeze blew tendrils about her delicate face. She had a wonderfully warm, inviting smile which immediately made my heart begin to pound out of my chest and I thought to myself this gorgeous creature must be an angel sent from heaven.

I must have been thinking out loud because Billy pretending to fan himself said, "Now that's one hot chick!"

Charlie chimed in as he pushed his wheelchair as fast as the wheels would turn, "Amen, brother…she's definitely a hottie!"

It wouldn't be long before I realized why people say not to judge a book by its cover.

"Hey, four eyes…yeah you, shorty. You gonna eat all those apples by yourself or may I have one? So where are you guys off to…a Halloween party or something?" She looked at Troubadour as she said, "I see the big guy still has his costume on."

Charlie was the first to say what we were all thinking, "Kind of rude, aren't you?"

The girl stuck her nose in the air and said, "Like I care what some cripple thinks." She added, "I see you didn't take my advice and run did you. Like, I've never seen so many hornet stings!"

"Not only are you rude but you're mean, too" Billy said.

Jumping to her feet the girl responded, "Well, what do we have here? You're such a loser…hasn't anyone told you Goth is so not in anymore? Oh, I get it…you're trying to make a statement, aren't you?" she smirked.

If Cindy hadn't acted quickly and grabbed the apple from her brother's hand, he might have thrown it right between the pretty girl's ocean blue eyes.

Troubadour stepped up, put his hand out, and said, "Thanks for the warning back there with those hornets."

The girl refused to shake Troubadour's hand and said snidely, "Sure. So big guy, what circus did you escape from?" She looked Troubadour over warily.

Troubadour merely smiled warmly at her and said, "This is Cindy and her older brother Billy."

Then Charlie held out a hand to shake. "Glad to meet you, I think. I'm Charlie and this guy is Bobby," he said as he pulled me towards the front of his chair.

"My friends call me B.C." I said shyly as I handed her the nicest apple I had.

Billy quipped, "Right... like you have friends!"

To our surprise Cindy reached out one of her small, soft hands with the other firmly held in her brother's hand, and said shyly, "What's your name? Would you like to be my new friend?"

The girl reluctantly took Cindy's hand and said, "Sure, I could use a friend. My name is Tiffany Johnson."

Billy and I were elbowing each other to get a little closer to Tiffany. Being nudged from behind, I said, "What brings you so deep into the woods?"

In between bites of her apple Tiffany replied, "This place is as good as any other if you don't fit in anywhere else."

Troubadour said, "Where do you live?"

Tiffany's voice turned from a smile to a frown and her voice began to crack, "It's none of your business where I live or anything else about me. You guys are probably just like everyone else in my life. You act like you care, but when you get right down to it, you don't. Matter of fact, after awhile you'll probably toss me out like yesterday's newspaper. So why should I believe you guys are any different?"

I said, "I'm sorry you feel that way. I'm just concerned that maybe your parents might be worried about your safety out here by yourself."

"You're hysterical," laughed Tiffany slapping her knee with her hand. "Where did you guys find this comedian? If it didn't hurt so much I would laugh. Both of my parents are very successful investment bankers. My father is the CEO of his own investment firm and is never home and cheats on my mother every chance he gets. My mother has turned into a pill-popping alcoholic because of it. I don't even think my parents know or care if I'm alive or dead!" Cindy's face contorted as she added, "They didn't even send me a birthday card for my birthday!"

Tiffany turned away from us, but we could tell she was beginning to cry. She tried to put on a brave face for us and continued, "I don't really have much of a home. Both of my parents travel all the time and are barely there. As a matter of fact, they are both vacationing in Hawaii right now and don't even know I'm gone yet."

"Why didn't you go with them?" I asked.

Tiffany replied, "I wasn't invited! I've been raised by three different nannies in the last seven years. The only time my parents show any interest in me at all is when they have to stop their busy schedules to come bail me out of trouble."

Cindy looked at her brother signaling him to do something so Billy asked clumsily, "What kind of trouble?"

Tiffany rolled her eyes and responded, "Driving without a license twice, shoplifting three times, and my favorite—underage drinking and public intoxication. That one got me three months locked up in Rehab! Have you ever wondered why you're alive and if anyone out there cares? I'm sorry…I really didn't mean to dump all that on you guys. I just needed to vent a little, I guess."

Charlie said, "Well, Tiffany, you sound like a perfect candidate to come along with us to find the Dark Hole. It's where teens like us, who don't fit in anywhere, can go to put an end to our pain. It's where no one can ever hurt us ever again. So what do you say, Tiffany? Want to come along?"

I hoped to myself that Tiffany would say "yes." She placed her arm around Charlie's shoulders and said, "Sure, count me in. It's kind of funny that you guys happened along when you did. I had a similar conversation with a snake named Damien last night. He's kind of cool, especially with those sunglasses of his."

I put my hand out in front of me and said to the gang. "Put them here." Then Billy and his sister, followed by Charlie and finally Tiffany, stacked their hands upon each other's and I shouted "Repeat after me...One for all and all for one!" as Troubadour looked on.

Then we all proceeded to repeat it over and over...trying to really believe the words we were saying. I noticed a tear fall down Troubadour's cheek, as he saw and understood the deep despair and hurt in each one of us. He briefly looked up to heaven as if to say, "Help, please."

Troubadour then said, "Maybe this would be a good time to consider what this journey actually means." He went on to suggest that we turn around and head back home.

We all looked at each other, then turned and looked at Troubadour. Without a word, we knew that he knew that we were more determined than ever to stay on our course until completion. We decided this would be a perfect place to end the journey for the day so we bedded down in the tall grass for some much needed sleep.

CHAPTER 7
Bridge of Hope

Exhausted from yesterday's travels and still a bit groggy, I woke to a low whisper coming from a tree directly behind where I was sleeping.

"Pssst, pssst, pssst! Hey, kid! For crying out loud already, WAKE UP!" which was really quite annoying.

Yawning and rubbing my eyes, I finally responded, "For crying out loud, Damien, what do you want?"

Damien quickly put the end of his tail over my mouth and whispered, "Keep your voice down, kid...you know the big guy needs his beauty sleep."

Yawning once again, I lay back on the grass for a couple more minutes of shut-eye. Next thing I know, just like when my mother couldn't get me up for school, I felt a tap, tap, tap on my forehead.

Getting a bit perturbed I sat up and said, "What?!"

Now eye-to-eye with that pesky reptile, he harped, "What's the matter, Bobby? You don't want to sleep the rest of your life away, do you?"

I reached for my glasses and put them on. "This had better be important." I said wishing for some snake repellent.

Damien put his tail across his forehead and replied, "That's what I get for trying to encourage you to be all you can be." Reappearing from behind his tail and making sure I was still watching, Damien added, "I'm kind of tired, too, Bobby. But here I am, taking time out of my busy morning, to stop by and tell you that I alone have confidence in you to do this."

Damien put his tail around my shoulders, "I have faith in you, boy. Now lead your new friends to their promised land of no more pain. After all, aren't you an Eagle Scout?" Damien uncoiled himself from around my shoulders and silently disappeared into the thick brush.

I was so tired from our travels that I fell back asleep for a few more minutes—but it wasn't meant to be. I was re-awakened by nature's alarm clock, a symphony of assorted sounds that the forest was broadcasting. Everything in the woods was still wet from last night's dew, including me.

Seeing how I was awake and up first, I decided to survey the lay of the land. As I followed the path, I watched several squirrels playing tag in the trees. Before I had realized it, the path had come to an abrupt end.

Directly before me was a giant ravine that dropped at least a hundred feet or more, straight down to a fast-moving river. On either side of the ravine were jagged rocks that led up to an old rickety bridge…one of those creepy hanging bridges like you see in the movies.

The wind cut through the valley making a whistling sound as it made the ancient bridge sway back and forth. I noticed that it was missing several wooden slats and a chill went up my spine as I became concerned for the safety of my friends.

I was surprised when I turned around to find the whole gang already standing there behind me mapping out a strategy to conquer the bridge so that we could be on our way.

After careful consideration and more than a little discussion between us, we decided to put our plan into motion. Troubadour grabbed the handles of Charlie's chair and began slowly pushing Charlie across the narrow bridge. Every movement was precise as he masterfully maneuvered the wheelchair towards the other end of the decaying bridge.

I followed along behind Troubadour and Charlie very carefully. With each foot of progress, the bridge screeched and cracked under our weight and that of Charlie's chair. Dust and splinters went fluttering down to the bottom of the ravine like confetti. Some of the looser slats gave way and dropped like bombs into the river below.

Drops of perspiration ran off my head as we inched our way across, further and further. My heart was in my throat until the three of us made it safely to the other side. With even more slats missing, it would be more dangerous than ever for Tiffany, Cindy, and Billy to cross the swaying deathtrap.

Billy started out first, followed by his sister. Tiffany followed them, bringing up the rear. Slowly they inched their way across the old bridge while Charlie and I shouted encouragement to them. Without warning, the crumbling slat that Billy was standing on gave way under his weight, causing him to crash through the planks. Billy was dangling by his armpits holding on for dear life. Cindy grabbed her brother's shirt and was frantically screaming for help.

Panic-stricken, Tiffany was yelling with the same intensity for Cindy to hold on while she desperately clung to the draw ropes, which held the bridge up as it swayed in the wind.

Not to be left out, I got involved in the ruckus by letting out a high-pitched scream when Charlie rolled back on my foot with the wheel of his chair. All of the shouting was deafening as it echoed up and down the deep valley walls.

Troubadour started towards Billy. He went as fast as he could without causing an even bigger problem than we already had. After a few long minutes, Troubadour reached Billy and his sister. He calmly asked Cindy to stop screaming, and had Tiffany take the young girl's hand, motioning them to the other side where I was waiting. Cindy kept one hand in Tiffany's and one on the rope as they cautiously headed for the end of the bridge.

While waiting for the girls to join us, I noticed Damien, that cunning old snake, had wrapped himself around the ropes that held the bridge in place. He was whispering to Billy, "Just let go. You know you want to. Your pain can end for you right now! Come on you, chicken," Damien hissed.

I hurried over to help Tiffany bring a reluctant Cindy to solid ground. It touched my heart seeing Tiffany more concerned about Cindy's safety than her own. When we reached the rocky ground where Charlie sat, I knew that we were safe.

I looked back and saw Troubadour grab the back of Billy's shirt and give it one mighty pull. Soon Billy was free and on his feet again. A short time later, Troubadour and Billy joined us and we all came together in a celebration hug.

It was nice to know we were all safe and sound—together again. If you think about it, this made absolutely no sense. We were on a journey to find the Dark Hole to end it all. Yet here we were in a jubilant and joyful reunion celebrating life!

Shielding his eyes from the overwhelming brightness of the sun with his large paw, Troubadour suggested that we make our way down the deep ravine to get some cool, refreshing water from the river below.

"Eeeew," Cindy said. "I'm not going to drink from a dirty, muddy river."

Patting Cindy on the top of the head Troubadour added, "I'm trying to keep you guys from becoming dehydrated."

Removing my hat and wiping the perspiration off my forehead, I decided to put in my two-cents, "The spring water that runs into that river will be as clean as the water from your faucet at home— minus a few ugly insects and all those creepy crawly, unseen things."

Charlie broke in adding, "Bugs or not, I haven't had anything to drink in two days and I'm really thirsty." Pointing to the bottom of the ravine he said, "There's no way I can get my chair down there, though."

Smiling from ear to ear, the big furry creature slid both of his enormous paws under Charlie's hips and with one powerful heave, lifted Charlie's helpless body onto his broad shoulders like a sack of potatoes. "Are you ready?" Troubadour asked.

With both of his arms dangling at Troubadour's side, Charlie responded, "I guess this problem has been solved."

Billy took his sister's hand and we all started on our long descent down to the bottom of the ravine. We carefully traveled down the rocky ledges just beneath the old, broken-down bridge where Billy had almost lost his life. After a couple hours or more, we finally reached the bottom and rushed over to the river's edge. The sparkling blue water was crystal clear just like I thought it would be.

Excitedly pulling an empty water bottle from her treasured brown leather bag, Tiffany yelled, "Hey guys, look what I've got!"

Putting my hand in the air for a high five, I responded, "Way to go, Tiffany!" Ms. Gorgeous rolled her beautiful blue eyes and left me hanging as was her character. Billy smirked and forcefully slapped my open hand, leaving it to sting while he found a nearby boulder to sit on.

Cindy and her newfound friend took turns drinking from the water bottle with their eyes tightly closed, savoring the cold water. Charlie rolled onto his stomach next to the water's edge and began lapping the water like a thirsty animal. With his eyes fixated on a group of trees located in the marshes next to the river bank, Troubadour dipped his big paws into the river bringing the water slowly to his lips. He reminded me of a well-trained warrior on guard duty.

Finished, Cindy tossed the empty bottle over to me to refill. With my thirst finally quenched, I lobbed the community water bottle over to where Billy was sitting. Billy gulped down the rest of the water and refilled the well-used water bottle, returning it back to its original owner full of water.

Tiffany warmly whispered to Billy, "Thanks," and winked at him.

Noticing Tiffany's innocent flirtation with Billy, my temperature arose. I jealously blurred out, "Shouldn't we be on our way, Troubadour?"

Apparently that was the cue Troubadour needed to lift Charlie up with one strong hand in a fireman's carry. You would have thought Charlie had just gotten a free ticket for a carnival ride or something, only it was on the gentle giant's shoulder. As usual, Billy grabbed his sister's hand and followed Troubadour with Charlie in tow up the side of the jagged cliff.

Making the first ledge of the rough terrain, I turned around to offer Tiffany a helping hand. Much to my surprise, she was in the process of swallowing three little white pills which she had taken from a pill bottle hidden in a side-pouch of her brown bag.

Embarrassed from her secret being discovered, she angrily snapped, "What's your problem?" Infuriated by the look of disapproval on my face, Tiffany shoved past me in hyper-drive to put as much distance between us as possible. That left me to bring up the rear for the first time on this journey.

After several more hours of climbing, we were back to where we had begun, except for a few new scrapes, cuts, and bruises. The six of us had made it safely back up to the top of the ridge by mid-afternoon.

The temperature on the ridge was dramatically different than it was earlier that morning. In fact, the heat was so intense it felt like we were in a sauna—not that I have ever been in a sauna, but I have read that the temperature ranges between 150 to 194 degrees Fahrenheit. I decided I would keep this trivia to myself, though.

Pulling a scrunchie from her bag, Tiffany put her long damp hair into a ponytail and said, "I don't think my tanning bed at home is any hotter than this, even turned up all the way."

Noticing that Troubadour didn't seem bothered by the heat, I asked "Aren't you hot, big guy?" while wiping the sweat from the lenses of my glasses again.

"I've learned to be content in whatever state I find myself in."

Charlie interrupted and added, "Me too, Troubadour, but the rubber on my ride is starting to melt." His humor got a laugh out of all of us and helped us to keep on going.

We really needed to pick up the pace to make up for the time lost in the ravine. We hurried along the path, stopping only long enough to pick some plump blackberries that we saw on the way.

The hot afternoon sun was high in the cloudless sky, letting us know we had a very long and steamy day still ahead of us.

We walked for what seemed like hours and saw nothing but trees, trees, and more trees—as far as you could see. Their shade was much appreciated, though—we would have burnt to a crisp without it since the temperature only seemed to get much hotter as the day went on. The relentless heat did its best to zap our strength or what was left of it.

If this wasn't miserable enough, the red-winged blackbirds flying above us dropped nasty presents on us from time to time. Let me tell you, there's nothing like cleaning berry-colored bird poop out of your hair without any water!

None of us have bathed for days and it was starting to tell. The clothes that we were wearing stuck to us as if something had glued them onto our backs. We were dirty, grimy and downright nasty smelling but we were doing the best we could under the extreme weather conditions.

It was our determination to find the Dark Hole that kept us going. We walked in silence with the only interruption being an occasional squeak from the wheels on Charlie's wheelchair.

With our water supply depleted, we were all getting pretty thirsty and Troubadour suggested we venture off the path to find water and a place to make camp. He gave us each some chores to get the camp ready for a good night's sleep, then disappeared into a thick grove of pine trees without a word.

Tiffany, Cindy, and I gathered wood for a fire. Billy and Charlie found some good tree limbs and old vines that we could use to make a little shelter. We all worked hard together to make our night as comfortable as possible.

Proud of our accomplishments and with the final inspection complete, we sat down together around the unlit campfire which would be needed for light rather than warmth.

A northern breeze rustled through the leaves on the trees, providing us much needed relief from the sweltering heat. The only other noise we could hear was an occasional growl from one of our hungry stomachs.

Breaking the unusual silence of the forest Charlie announced, "I could eat a horse."

Agreeing with Charlie wholeheartedly, I chimed in, "Me, too!"

Catching a rather large beetle from mid-air, Billy asked, "What about this?"

Swatting Billy's arm allowing the insect to escape, Tiffany squealed, "Yuck! Are you nuts?"

Leaning back against her brother's shoulder Cindy whispered, "I'm thirsty, Billy."

Unable to help his sister, Billy said, "Sorry Sis, we're all thirsty. It's too bad we couldn't find any water."

Reaching inside her hand bag Tiffany pulled out the empty plastic water bottle and dropped it to the ground. "Sorry girl, we finished the last of the water hours ago."

Not feeling too optimistic myself, I tried to keep my focus on the grove of pine trees that swallowed up Troubadour, hoping for his quick return. "I wonder where Troubadour is…" I muttered.

Jumping to his feet and accidentally knocking my hat off, Billy blurted out, "Maybe Troubadour got smart and deserted us."

Dusting off my hat and putting it back on my head, I angrily snapped, "You're stupid and don't know anything!"

Removing his driving gloves, Charlie said, "You're right, Billy. The big guy probably got tired of carrying around my useless, good-for-nothing body."

Getting up in Charlie's face, I yelled in opposition, "That's not true and you know it!"

With the same intensity Charlie shouted back, "Then where is he, Bobby? Huh?"

Taking off her shoes, Tiffany declared in a calm, collected voice, "My little delusional traveling companion, sit down and relax before you blow a gasket." Rubbing a blister on her heel, she continued, "Besides, Bobby Cooper, you know as well as I do someone or something will always let you down in the end."

49

"Not Troubadour! I protested, "He promised to come with us to the Dark Hole…" Needing my space, I found a different tree away from the others so I could pout in peace.

I watched the empty water bottle fly past my head hearing my so-called new friends laughing at me. I thought how incredibly ironic life would be if we would perish from dehydration or starvation before we reached the Dark Hole to end it all. And at that moment it didn't matter how, I just wanted the laughing to stop.

What a wonderful surprise it was to see Troubadour returning back to camp! On his right shoulder, he was carrying a giant bunch of swamp roots that looked like muddy softballs tied to the ends of long, slimy, black weeds. In his left hand was the largest line of freshly-caught rainbow trout that I had ever seen.

He was singing his little jingle, "Walking in love, walking in the light, every morning, noon and night." I knew that we would eat well tonight thanks to Troubadour.

Using only the tip of his finger, Troubadour lit the campfire we had arranged without a match. Tiffany looked at me with amazement and before she could speak I said, "Don't even ask."

Troubadour settled down next to the large pile of disgusting looking swamp roots. Pulling a small three-inch pocket knife from his breast pocket, Troubadour grabbed a root and made a one-inch incision on one end, and a three-inch slit on the other end. Putting the root in the palm of his mighty paw, he squeezed the nasty, smelly thing until it started dripping some white, milky liquid.

Sitting down next to Troubadour, Tiffany handed him her empty water bottle saying, "You might need this."

"Thanks," Troubadour responded.

With nothing else to do, I decided to hold the water bottle under the root to catch the root juice so Troubadour could use both his paws to squeeze. After refilling the empty bottle six times, Troubadour hoisted the last root over his head, squeezing with all his might until his jaws were filled with the white root juice.

Standing to his feet and holding the ugly remains of the root out in front of him, Troubadour proclaimed, "Swamp roots and humans have a lot in common..."

Being quite attractive, Tiffany said sarcastically, "Gee whiz, thanks, Troubadour..."

Poking at the fire with a stick, Billy taunted, "Well it does look like Bobby if you ask me."

Slapping Billy in the back of his head and telling him to shut up, I asked Troubadour, "How's that?"

Troubadour answered my question by saying, "The great creator placed hidden treasures into each swamp root and every human being."

Throwing another log on the fire, Troubadour continued, "Humans tend to focus all their attention and judgment on outward appearances, never investing one moment of thought towards the value and beauty of what is inside."

Holding the ugly remains of the swamp root over the open fire Troubadour exclaimed, "There is no outward beauty to this swamp root, yet you've all tasted of its true inner value, and it was good!"

Standing to her feet and stretching Cindy said, "It was quite tasty, if you ask me."

"It had a sweet taste," added Tiffany.

Laying a flat rock next to the camp fire to clean the fish on, I added, "It quickly quenched your thirst, too."

Dropping the swamp root remains into the camp fire Troubadour said, "Before its inner beauty can be seen and appreciated to the fullest, as with each of you, it first must go into the fire!"

At first nothing happened. Then all of a sudden, the flames of the camp fire shot five feet into the air as the fire became alive and began to dance in a prism of spectacular colors...First in bright oranges, then in vivid blues, contrasted by brilliant greens, and ending in crimson red. With each color change, a new fragrance filled the air. The aromas were so awesome, similar to lilac, then cinnamon, and finally ginger.

Breaking some twigs up and throwing them into the fire, I began to wonder what Troubadour meant when he implied, "Before the inner beauty of a man can be revealed, he must first walk through the fire."

It wasn't long before Troubadour had the fish cleaned, cut, and cooking. The delicious aroma of fish roasting over an open fire filled the air. I don't know if that was the best fish I had ever eaten, or if hunger had just made it seem that way—either way, we ate like a bunch of pigs.

Since we were all stuffed, we kicked back to relax, settling in for another long night in the woods. A pack of wolves howled to one another in the distance. With the glow of the campfire on our faces, we all sprawled out around the campfire in the small clearing.

We watched the billowing smoke twist high into the sky in a swirling motion. It was interweaving itself with the limbs of the thick, tall trees creating a canopy over us. Peacefully we sat around the fire, enjoying its comforting warmth and the new friendships we had found in our alliance.

Billy sat on my right trying to knock my hat off with a long stick. On my left, Charlie was sprawled out on the ground pulling at some dried grass. Tiffany, sitting between Billy and Troubadour, was rearranging her ponytail, now shimmering in the light of the fire. On Troubadour's other side, Cindy was braiding bright red beads into long strands of his reddish brown hair.

Troubadour was directly opposite me on the other side of the fire. He looked more confident and majestic than ever. "No wonder the lion is known as the king of the jungle," I thought. My thoughts drifted to what the morning might bring while being seduced by familiar voices in my head. "I've never feared dying, but living scares me to death!" I thought.

It seemed Troubadour must have been reading my mind as he began a new conversation with a question, "Is the Dark Hole really the answer to your problems? Perhaps you might consider another..."

I interrupted him, "Troubadour, there's no way you will ever understand unless you have experienced the pain that we have. I mean, have you ever felt the pain of rejection or the hurt from always being overlooked?"

"Well…" responded Troubadour.

Interrupting Troubadour, with anger in his voice, Billy added, "Or have you ever been branded as a loser or failed at everything you've tried? Including protecting your sister?"

Becoming frustrated, Troubadour said, "Well no…"

Tiffany stood to her feet and yelled, "What gives you the right to tell us what to do?"

"I was only suggesting that…," replied Troubadour.

"For crying out loud, my parents didn't even remember my last birthday," ranted Tiffany. "Can you understand the pain in that?"

Before Troubadour could answer, Charlie said, "Do people stare at you because of your handicap, thinking you're defective? I go to the bathroom in a bag." Charlie gulped and finished, "I'm not any good to anybody…I'm useless."

With tears streaming down Cindy's face she said, "Have you ever felt so dirty and ugly, afraid to go to sleep because of the nightmares…or worse yet, an unwelcome visitor in the night?" Cindy closed her eyes and insisted, "I can't go home! I just can't go home!"

Finally Troubadour got his opportunity to answer our questions. "You're right—there's no way I could understand unless I have suffered like you all have. But what I do know is this… I don't believe you really want to end it all. You just want the pain to end."

Leaning forward he continued, "Please consider this…maybe your emotional pain is a consequence of believing lies. Perhaps you just need to change the way you think and what you think about…with truth replacing lies."

Throwing more wood on the fire, Troubadour added, "Maybe you worry too much about what others think of you. Perhaps how you perceive yourself should be more important." Pausing to look at each one of us in the eye, he said, "Maybe you should change your focus."

Billy angrily stirred the fire with a stick and said, "Troubadour, you just don't get it! It hurts too much and those voices in my head constantly try to control my thoughts."

With compassion in Troubadour's voice, he said, "Billy, if you could only see past your circumstances and see the truth...it would stop the voices."

Cindy crawled into Troubadour's lap and put her head against his big, strong chest. Troubadour put his arms around her and held her close to him. He continued, "The things which are seen are earthly but the things which are not seen are everlasting."

Still angry, Tiffany looked at Troubadour and said, "What on earth are you talking about?"

Troubadour smiled, and then said, "Some things we see cannot change, but some things which we cannot see have an opportunity to still change. Before anyone else can love you, you must learn to love yourself." With that said, he suggested we get some sleep because the morning would be here before we knew it.

The rest of the night I stared at the thousands of stars which littered the night sky thinking about all that Troubadour had said until I finally drifted to sleep.

CHAPTER 8
It Looks Like Rain

The next morning, after much tossing and turning—and a nightmare or two, I was awakened by the song of a whippoorwill. I laid there thinking that it's so funny that the bird's name sounds just like its song. The sunbeams beating down on my face promised that it was going to be another scorching hot day.

Since I was an early riser, I decided to take a walk before the others started stirring. I hadn't gotten very far down the trail when suddenly Damien appeared, curled around an old silver maple tree, holding an umbrella over his head with his tail. His familiar sunglasses were still firmly in place, hiding his enormous eyes.

"Hi, Squirt, looks like rain doesn't it?" Damien leaned back against the tree, slowly closed the umbrella and hung it on a nearby branch.

Exasperated, I threw my hands up in the air, "Oh great, now you're a weather man! There's not a rain cloud in the sky…" I said as I peered up into the clear, blue sky.

Taking off his sunglasses, revealing his dark green eyes, Damien cautioned, "Well, I tried to warn you."

I laughed nervously and shouted back at him, "It's going to be a good day for me and my friends! You go on. We'll be fine, but thanks for your concern…"

Hissing he said, "Sure, kid. By the way, where is your big furry friend? It warms my heart to see you guys becoming so close lately. It's too bad it's all a bunch of hooey. I mean, come on now, building self- esteem and confidence through positive self-worth?

Sounds good, sure, but it doesn't work! It only produces false hope. What I offer you is self-focus and self-control."

After cleaning his sunglasses and putting them back on his head, Damien slid his long slender body around mine and lifted me several inches off the ground. "Take control of your life, kid. You got it?" Damien's eyes met mine and that look haunted me.

A little hesitant I stammered, "I got it!"

"I hope so, kid." touching his tail to his chest, Damien continued to say, "So take it from an expert, you need to take control of your life. Remember what your coach told you last season? When the going gets tough, the tough get going. So get going and finish your course. Do your miserable, pathetic little selves a favor and see it through to the end."

Then Damien slithered away as I heard him say, "Still looks like rain to me," and he laughed.

Damien's forecast of wet weather seemed weird to me. My logical mind said it was very unlikely to happen since there wasn't a cloud in the sky—but I couldn't shake the uneasy feeling in my gut.

I started back down the trail to meet the others so we could continue on our journey to the Dark Hole. As I walked, I began to notice that the noisy woods had become abnormally quiet. Like a magician's trick, the sun mysteriously disappeared right before my eyes. The clear sky had suddenly turned quite dark and was filled with ominous black thunderheads.

The leaves of the trees turned right side up to catch the rain. The eerie stillness engulfed me as all of nature prepared for the drastic change. You could feel it in the air. A strong wind now tore through the trees with reckless abandon. Without warning, lightning began to flash across the sky and loud thunder rumbled behind it.

It started at first with one drop of rain, then another, and another. Then the heavens opened up with a vengeance. It began to rain buckets and buckets of water. It was raining so hard it was getting difficult to see the path directly in front of me. The once solid ground was soon turning into a large pit of mud. Nature was in the process of revealing its dreadful fury—full of power and destruction.

Wide eyed and frightened, I reached the others who were huddled together under what was left of the shelter that we had built. As soon as I joined them, Troubadour suggested we get out of the valley and head for higher ground.

Before we could take a step, we heard what sounded like a freight train in a tunnel. Suddenly, we became terrified as we looked up and saw not a train—but a huge wall of water heading straight for us.

It was knocking down anything that dared get in its path, sucking it up like a giant vacuum cleaner and then spitting it back out in a rush of fallen tree limbs, rocks and mudslides.

We knew we couldn't outrun the wave so we decided to all hold on to the large oak trees around us, hoping to ride out the storm. That tsunami-like wave of water hit my tree with such an unbelievable force that it nearly ripped my arms off my body. The power of the incessant rushing water was too much for us to battle.

Cindy was the first to lose her hold on the tree she was clinging to, followed by her older brother, Billy. Troubadour voluntarily released his tight grip on his oak tree to help rescue Billy and his screaming sister.

Tiffany somehow was able to wrap her arms around my waist and was frantically trying to hold on with all her strength. Swallowing another mouthful of water, she screamed. "Help me, Bobby…Please!"

I tightly wrapped my legs around the tree hoping to free up my hands to help Tiffany, and yelled, "Give me your hand!"

Knowing she couldn't hang on much longer, I composed myself. With new-found confidence, I reached down and tried to grab her wrists with both hands, while trying desperately to hang onto the tree with my failing legs.

The current made it impossible to accomplish both tasks at the same time. Tiffany's face said it all—her beautiful blue eyes closed as I watched her lifeless body disappear into the white caps of the murky waters. With my heart breaking and my tears making it hard to see, I frantically tried to hang on to my tree trunk.

Memories of all of my past failures and defeats flooded my mind. With the last ounce of energy drained from my weary body, I screamed "I can't believe I couldn't get this one thing right." Too exhausted to hang on any longer, I became the next victim of the raging waters.

My body went in directions I didn't think possible. Head over heels I rolled, desperately trying to keep my head above the dirty water. My body bounced and ricocheted off of anything it came in contact with—it was as if I had become a human pinball game. I swallowed mouthful after mouthful of dirty water while I urgently tried to grab onto any floating debris in sight.

The last thing I remembered seeing was Charlie and his wheelchair being swallowed up by the water's rage and spun around like they were caught in the spin-cycle of a giant washing machine. Now I know how surfers must feel when they lose control of the wave and their body is pounded by the surf.

As fast as the nightmare began, it was over. I clung to the rock which had stopped my body with a final thud. After lying there for a few minutes, I began to check my limbs for broken bones and slowly climbed to my feet—everything seemed to be in good working order. Unfortunately, my glasses didn't fare as well, but were still wearable.

Struggling over to the spot where Charlie's chair had come to rest upside down, I called out "Are you alright, Charlie?" Charlie was working hard to sit upright and straighten out his twisted legs. With the wound on the back of his head reopened and bleeding, Charlie jokingly replied, "I think so but I have no feeling in my legs!"

"Funny, Charlie," I said, "but you might not have such a sense of humor once you see your wheelchair." His wheelchair had come to rest against a rock and was missing one wheel entirely, the other wheel still spinning around and around.

Charlie tried to get the mud out of his hair as he said, "Well, I definitely made out better than my chair. Have you found anyone else?"

Covered in mud myself, I responded, "Not yet. Since it doesn't look like you're in any real danger, I'll go and try to find the others, okay?"

Charlie leaned against the tree and smiled, "Sure go, I'll be fine."

So I began to walk in small circles calling out the names of my fallen comrades. "Billy, Cindy, Troubadour, Tiffany!!! Can anyone hear me?"

After the third time around, I heard Troubadour's familiar voice call back to me, "Over here, Bobby!" I sloshed towards Troubadour's voice, calling out every so often to make sure I was still heading in the right direction.

When I finally reached Troubadour, he had already applied first aid to Billy and his frightened sister. Billy had a small head wound and Cindy had a bandage made from her brother's shirt around her leg, just over the knee.

As I approached Troubadour, he asked, "Do you know where the others are?"

I pointed towards where I had just left Charlie. Out of breath I said, "Charlie's over there, leaning up against a tree."

Troubadour, with a worried look on his face, asked if I needed first aid. I shook my head "no" but added, "Charlie's chair has seen its last day, though."

Troubadour sent Billy, Cindy and me back to wait with Charlie while he went to look for Tiffany. Billy carried his sister in his arms as we walked. At that moment, I realized how fortunate we were to have Troubadour with us on this journey. I wondered to myself, where we would be right now without his guidance and watchful eye. I also wondered why no one had asked Troubadour what he was doing out here in the forest.

An hour later, Troubadour returned with Tiffany high up on his mighty shoulders, both were singing his little jingle. "Walking in love, walking in the light, every morning, noon and night." Other than a few scratches and a bruise here and there, Tiffany looked in pretty good shape.

We all sat there figuratively licking our wounds trying to recover. Everyone was covered in mud from head to toe. I couldn't help but think how really lucky we all were not to be seriously hurt or even killed—and I was sincerely relieved that we were all together again.

It had stopped raining but a heavy mist began to cover the forest floor. Pools of muddy water full of rubble and debris covered the area.

For some strange reason, Tiffany now found the whole incident to be ridiculously funny and her laugh echoed throughout the forest. If we weren't in so much pain, we might have joined her in her nervous breakdown.

The blue-gray skies gave way to the sun in its full strength. It provided us with much needed heat to dry our clothes out or what was left of them anyway. While I was sitting there staring into space, I remembered the last thing Damien had said, "Looks like rain to me."

The longer we sat there, we noticed we were becoming more than a little stiff. Billy complained of a sore neck and I noticed my lower back was developing some pain as well.

Tiffany threw her hands up and said, "What a bunch of whiney butts. You think you have problems, look at my beautiful hair!" Tiffany put both her hands in my face and let out a scream. "Ooooh! I broke two of my nails!"

Billy wiped a little blood from a cut on his left elbow and said, "I can't remember a time in my life that I have seen so many losers assembled together in one place, at one time. I can't believe we can't even get this right. You would think something as simple as following a path until you reached a place named the Dark Hole to jump into would be easy. It shouldn't take that much brain power or effort unless we really are the goofballs, losers and mess ups everyone says we are."

Troubadour pulling globs of mud from his mane, challenged, "If you ask me, I think you guys need to focus on the positive and not so much of the negative." Wiping his muddy paws on the green grass he continued, "You guys shouldn't be so critical of yourselves or each other."

Cindy threw a hunk of mud at her brother and hit him right above his right ear.

Billy wiped his ear and then his mud-covered hand on the back of her head and said, "Troubadour, how could we possibly find anything positive in this disaster?"

"Smack, smack, smack," rang out as Troubadour sat in a dirty mud puddle banging his two gigantic size-eighteens together. He was trying to coax some stubborn mud from the soles of his large, filthy sneakers which now looked like two small speedboats repetitively running into each other. Troubadour paused a moment then said, "How about the fact that you guys work very well together. You always help each other out. Those are both positive truths."

I thought about what Troubadour had said as I scraped at the caked-on mud covering the bottom of my water-logged sneakers. Wanting him to know that I understood, I jumped into the conversation, "I get it…The glass is either half empty or half full depending on your perspective…Right, Troubadour?"

"Exactly," confirmed Troubadour.

Wiping some grime from her muddy face, Cindy frowned as she said, "When it comes to people like us, the glass is definitely half empty." Taking a long, deep breath she continued, "I mean, look at us…" She rose to her feet and held out her dirty, wet shirt. "We can't even get this right."

Sitting there in a foot of mud, I watched Tiffany frantically searching along the tree lines to and fro, then in the bushes and undergrowth, behind rocks, fallen logs or anything that was stationary. I thought, "Man, she is acting weird." I watched her become more and more distressed so I shouted to her, "What are you looking for?"

All the noises in the woods went dead silent for a couple of seconds, and then Tiffany let loose a horrified scream repeating over and over "Where is my bag—where is my brown handbag?" Sweat drops dotted her pink cheeks as she held her muddy hands to her forehead.

Remembering the incident in the ravine, I knew with certainty the cause of Tiffany's meltdown. I stood up, surprised that my legs could hold me up, and stammered, "It's about those drugs, isn't it Tiffany?"

Sitting down on a fallen tree, Tiffany buried her head into her hands and commanded, "Don't you judge me, Bobby Cooper!"

Standing up with a shocked look on his dirty face, Billy replied, "Drugs…you? Whoa!"

Walking over to where Tiffany was sitting, Cindy sat down beside her stroking her dirty blonde hair with her hand and asked Tiffany, "Do you want help looking for your bag?"

Beginning to cry, Tiffany gasped and answered Cindy, "It doesn't matter anymore—it's all going to be over shortly, anyway."

Troubadour was surprisingly non-conversational. He just continued to clean mud out of his mane as he sang his favorite jingle. Occasionally, he would look up making eye contact with me, as if he wanted me to say or do something.

Unfortunately, speaking without thinking as I often do, I blurted out, "Tiffany, you're such a drama queen." This insult only made her cry harder. I don't know who gave me the worse look, Cindy or Troubadour. They say looks can kill, if that were true, there would be no reason to take one more step on this journey because I definitely would be dead! I just spread my arms and said, "What?"

I figured at that point the best thing I could do was get up and make myself useful by looking for Tiffany's bag. This was rather foolish because everything around us was covered in a foot of thick brown mud.

Returning with mud up to my knees, I looked in Tiffany's direction and mouthed, "I'm sorry," while holding my chest above my heart. Out of the corner of my eye, I noticed Billy watching me with disgust.

Troubadour and Billy put the final touches on the wooden stretcher that they had just masterfully designed and crafted out of rain-soaked tree limbs, branches, and vines. Satisfied with his handiwork, Billy stood up and gave Troubadour a nod of approval.

Then, kneeling down with his back to Cindy, he said, "Let's go, Sis." Cindy climbed up on his back as he muttered, "This is just about all of this love fest my stomach can handle."

He glared at me and said, "Are we moving on or what?"

I took the cue as a "yes" when Troubadour got to his feet and pulled the man-made wooden contraption up next to Charlie. Troubadour asked, "Did someone order a taxi?" Charlie rolled over onto the stretcher's matting and found a comfortable position for the long haul.

CHAPTER 9
The Calm before the Storm

We walked for the rest of the day, stopping only long enough to catch our breath and give our two "horses" some much needed rest. Although we'd been on the move most of the day, we hadn't covered much distance. The muddy trail was making the going pretty rough. The terrain was uneven, wet, and the path was covered in mud left over from the wall of water. Yet, bravely, we continued on our journey driven by a force we really couldn't see or understand.

After searching for the easiest route, we decided to follow the same god-forsaken trail that we were already on. Maneuvering Charlie's homemade stretcher was next to impossible because all of the mud, debris and tall grass covering the path.

Our journey troubles were compounded by the injuries we suffered earlier. Charlie had a deep head wound that had reopened and Cindy's right knee was badly swollen from her encounter with the wave of flood water. And then there was me.

With each and every excruciating step I took, the muscles in my lower back became stiffer and stiffer, making it hard at times to even catch my breath. But yet we marched on our way towards the Dark Hole, like well-trained soldiers determined to complete our secret mission.

We walked and walked and walked. Step after step, mile after mile, swatting at the blood-sucking mosquitoes which were dive-bombing our sore, battered and fatigued bodies.

Feeling brain-dead from heat-exhaustion and dehydration, I kept walking even though it was the hardest thing I had ever tried to do. Finally, exhausted and unable to take even one more step, I dropped to my knees holding my back in pain and cried out, "Sorry guys, I can't go any further!" Moving onto my rump, I removed my dirty sneakers and smelly socks revealing three new blisters between my toes.

With Charlie still fast asleep, Troubadour lowered the wooden stretcher slowly to the ground and said, "I was hoping we could make it to the river before nightfall."

His weary body collapsing in a heap onto the soft grass next to me, Billy gasped, "Troubadour, I've had it too. I'm done…"

Seconds later, Cindy limped up and fell face down next to her brother mumbling, "That makes three."

Charlie slowly opened his eyes, still half asleep. Using his fingers as a comb, he ran his hand through his hair a couple times with the hope of improving his appearance. Trust me it didn't work. But in Charlie's defense, nothing could have helped any of our appearances at that time.

We all smelled like a pair of dirty, stinky socks for lack of deodorant. All of our clothing was tattered and torn, not to mention covered with a layer of dried mud. I don't even want to think what our breath must have smelled like seeing how we hadn't brushed our teeth in days. Even beautiful Tiffany was starting to look pretty nasty.

Startled by a couple of squirrels chasing each other in the tree limbs just above my head, I stopped daydreaming long enough to realize Tiffany was nowhere to be seen. Standing to my feet slowly because of the stiff muscles in my back, I nervously asked, "Does anyone know where Tiffany is?"

Grabbing a low hanging branch of an old weeping willow tree, Billy hoisted himself to a sitting position and answered, "She was right behind Cindy and me."

Sitting up and looking down the trail, Cindy started screaming Tiffany's name at the top of her lungs. The noise sent hundreds of blackbirds into flight, scattering them in all directions. Before Cindy could get Tiffany's name out for the third time, Troubadour had jumped to his feet and began retracing our steps down the trail.

A few minutes later, that big lovable creature reappeared with Tiffany's trembling body snugly fixed in his enormous arms. The image of the two of them walking up the moonlit trail brought back memories of a day that I was searching through discarded materials at the city dump for go-cart parts, when I came across a beautifully crafted porcelain doll that had been tossed out with the rest of the junk. I had thought to myself, "How could anyone throw away such a precious gift?"

As the two of them drew closer, it reminded me of that day at the city dump, and I found myself asking the same question again, "How could Tiffany's parents throw away such a precious gift?"

Out of breath and with drops of perspiration dripping off the end of Troubadour's furry nose, I could see the concern not only in his sad, brown eyes—it was written all over his face.

But the worst part was the look of hopelessness on Tiffany's face. It was scary because the once strong-willed Tiffany was now a helpless, broken young girl. By the scent that filled the air it was obvious she had vomited on herself as well. It definitely wasn't a pretty picture.

Troubadour grunted once and said, "We need to find Tiffany some shelter immediately."

To my amazement when I looked up there it was. About fifty yards away, just to the left of Troubadour's right shoulder—a small glowing light suddenly appeared out of nowhere.

The light was coming from the mouth of a cave set deep into a cliff of a rocky ledge…Probably used by a family of hibernating black bears last winter. Troubadour tightened his hold on Tiffany's weak body and reluctantly headed towards the source of light. Cindy nodded enthusiastically in agreement.

Billy grabbed one pole of the stretcher and I rushed over to grab the other pole opposite of him. Together, with our combined strength, we began pulling the manmade stretcher with all our might. It reminded me of a team of plow horses trying to plow a muddy field…It was like pulling a wagon with no wheels.

With a lot of patience, effort, and sweat, we finally reached the mouth of the cave which was partially hidden by some heavy brush. Billy in his rush, got out of lock-step with me, and dropped his pole. This caused my pole to slip out of my grip, allowing Charlie and the stretcher to fall to the ground with a jarring thud.

Rubbing his head, Charlie looked up, "Gee whiz…thanks a lot, guys!"

Billy answered jokingly, "No problem, dude."

Troubadour entered the mouth of the cave first carrying Tiffany, followed closely by Billy and me. Cindy waited just outside the cave's door keeping Charlie company.

There, to my astonishment, was the source of the light—a perfectly built campfire. And as mystifying as that was, there were five one-gallon jugs full of fresh, clear water sitting next to the fire.

That wasn't all—sitting next to the water was a red and white striped tablecloth with the largest Welcome Wagon gift basket I've ever put my eyes on and it was overflowing with goodies. I rubbed my eyes in disbelief, thinking that I must be hallucinating!

Under the basket's big silver bow was the most tantalizing display of cheese and crackers, assorted nuts and cookies. It even had Mandarin oranges and tropical fruit. Puzzled I said, "I wonder who it belongs to?"

"Us," responded Billy, pulling off a hand-written note pinned to the wicker basket. He read it aloud to us:

I figured by now you guys might be pretty discouraged, so I wanted you to have these few gifts so you could be sure to finish your course.
Good luck,
Damien

With a disgusted look on his face, Troubadour lifted the basket off of the tablecloth with his free hand and sat it over on the ground next to the water. Then he lowered the moaning and incoherent Tiffany onto the center of the tablecloth.

Tiffany lay on the hard rock floor of the cave shaking uncontrollably with her knees doubled up to her chest in a fetal position. She was shivering and clinging tightly to a corner of the tablecloth now snugly nestled under her chin. Things looked pretty grim.

But even as concerned as I was for her, I started to choke and gag—Tiffany smelled like two-day-old spoiled hamburger and the rank odor began to fill the small cave. Strong puffs of disgusting vapors made our stomachs heave. I swear I almost vomited myself.

While Cindy prepared herself some food, Billy and I watched Tiffany who was now pulling off imaginary spiders from her sweat-drenched body…she was obviously hallucinating in her withdrawal from the drugs.

It was so painful listening to our friend mumble incoherently, "Leave me alone…just let me die." Which was just plain silly, since none of us could leave a fallen comrade behind.

Now it was my turn to eat. I stood next to the fire, swallowing handfuls of cashews without chewing. As I wolfed down some more snacks, I watched Cindy tenderly wiping Tiffany's matted hair from her forehead with a piece of cloth ripped from Billy's sweatshirt.

Looking like that, Tiffany reminded me of a helpless, newborn kitten. I was amazed that Cindy was able to leave the security of her hiding place long enough to help with Tiffany's needs.

Troubadour walked up, putting his big paw on my shoulder and said, "Isn't it nice that Cindy can put her own pain aside for the pain of another?"

Over the next day and a half we basically took care of Tiffany's needs, making sure she ate and drank whenever she was awake.

She couldn't look up without finding one of us staring back at her with a bit of food or shaking a plastic water jug in front of her.

Finally sitting up, Tiffany said, "Alright already!" Pulling her hair behind both her ears added, "I bet I look atrocious."

Still pale and with seriously dark circles and bags under her once beautiful blue eyes, I clumsily responded, "Well, I have seen you look better…"

Pushing me rather abruptly behind him, Billy winked at Tiffany and said, "You look a lot better than you did a couple days ago, girl!"

Tiffany smiled, and softly replied, "Thanks, Billy…" Then she took a bite of her saltine cracker.

Noticing Troubadour was nowhere to be seen—I grabbed a few of the mandarin oranges and went outside to look for him. He was just outside the opening of the cave, leaning against the rocks that made up the cave's outer wall. Sitting down next to Troubadour, I held out my hand offering him the last of the mandarin orange sections.

He sniffed at the orange and said, "No, thanks." He then pulled a funny Styrofoam-looking mushroom thing from his pocket and added, "I'll eat this."

"Yuck," I responded. "This has to be better tasting than whatever that thing is."

Troubadour leaned his head back on the rock and said, "Just because it looks good doesn't necessarily mean it's good for you. Beware of strangers bearing gifts."

Troubadour rose to his feet, smiled and said, "If Tiffany is ready, we should be on our way again." Jumping to my feet, I followed Troubadour into the cave to collect our friends and make ready to leave.

CHAPTER 10
The Dead End

We continued on our journey to the Dark Hole. Cindy and
Tiffany walked with their arms around each other. Billy and I
followed the girls and Troubadour pulled Charlie on the stretcher.

It wasn't too long before we were out of food and water again
but we continued on without worry.

Next thing we knew, Troubadour was leading us away from
the grassy path into the dense woods. Butterflies fluttered over the
fallen tree trunks, and bright red berries clung to the prickly shrubs.
We had not gone far when we heard what sounded like a rushing
river off in the distance.

Just then a flock of geese flew directly over our heads in a
tight V-formation, honking all the way. We followed the sound
of the river until we broke into a clearing. Raging before us was
a magnificent river still swollen out of its banks from the recent
storm.

Troubadour put Charlie carefully down on the ground as we
all stood there with our mouths hanging open wondering how on
earth we would be able to get past this latest obstacle. Closing my
mouth, I bit down on my lower lip to keep it from trembling as a
chill inched up my spine. Fear and dread gripped me.

Troubadour was the first to speak, fully understanding the
imminent danger that we would face if we tried to cross this river.
With concern in his voice he said, "Enough is enough. It's time to
reconsider putting an end to this journey and heading home before
someone really gets hurt."

Cindy grabbed her brother's hand and said, "Billy, please don't make me go home!" Billy hugged Cindy tightly and tried to reassure her that going home wasn't in his plans, either.

Tiffany, feeling a lot better physically, shouted out "Hey guys! Look over there!"

Much to our surprise, there in the middle of nowhere was a big, old fishing boat tied to a tree just beckoning us to take a closer look.

"Wonder who it belongs to," Charlie asked. Then answering his own question, "Who cares...finders' keepers, losers' weepers."

Troubadour jumped quickly in between us and the boat with his arms spread wide apart trying to become a road block. He shouted, "This is definitely a bad idea! Look how fast the current is moving. You'll never be able to steer the boat safely to the other bank...It's at least a half of a mile from here!"

Scratching behind his ear, he continued, "If you're not going home, at least let me find a safer route to cross the river."

Watching whole trees, roots, and all other debris being swept downstream by the intense surge of the murky blue flood water, I yelled "Maybe Troubadour is right. Perhaps we should try and find a safer way across this river...It's way too dangerous!"

Trying to be heard over the thunderous roar of the fast moving water, Charlie shouted out, "What are you...chicken?"

"I'm not afraid, I'm just being practical," I screamed.

Jokingly putting his hand on his hips and flapping his elbows like chicken wings, Billy squawked like a chicken and danced in circles around me.

Feeling my temper rising and my face turning three shades of red, spitting mad I picked up a polished gray stone off the river bank and threw it as hard as I could into the water—watching it skip three times over the white caps, finally disappearing into the currents of the raging waters.

Tired of arguing and eager to go, Billy picked up his sister and gently put her into the back of the boat. He then climbed slowly into the boat and took his place next to his sister, still flapping his elbows, pretending to be a chicken.

At Charlie's request, Troubadour—with reservations, placed him on the center board in the middle of the boat. He knew his legs were of no use but Charlie had excellent arm strength which would be needed if they were to have even a small chance of completing this overwhelming task.

Tiffany, petrified of water, stepped into the front of the boat and bravely slid to the starboard side with her eyes tightly shut.

I climbed into the boat to stop Billy's chicken imitation. While still having my doubts, I took my place at the helm, trying to reassure Tiffany that I would be there to protect her. "You're safe with me, Tiffany."

She just rolled her eyes and shook her head in disbelief as I shouted to Troubadour to shove off.

With a look of bewilderment on his face, Troubadour took his huge right paw placing it above his left eyebrow and jokingly saluted saying, "Aye-Aye, Captain!"

With Billy's foot pushing against the middle of my back, he mumbled under his breath, "More like Captain Chicken Little if you ask me."

Elbowing the ankle of his foot I said, "Nobody asked you."

"Shut up," Billy sneered.

"No, you shut up," I snapped.

Cindy scolded, "Boys!" Her rebuke quickly put an end to our squabbling.

Troubadour untied the boat from the maple tree while trying one last time to appeal to our better sense of judgment but it fell on deaf ears. He jumped into the nine-passenger fishing boat and took his seat in the center next to Charlie.

Together the two of them began to row with all their might as I barked out, "Row...Row...Row."

It didn't take us long to realize Troubadour was right again. The force of the fast moving river immediately turned the boat backwards. We began heading down the river in the wrong direction, totally out of control.

No matter how fast Troubadour and Charlie rowed, it didn't help…and if that wasn't bad enough, we started taking on water. The bottom of our boat was quickly filling up from the waves that pounded against and sloshed over the boat's sides. We started scooping the water with our hands as fast as we could but it didn't help and we began to sink fast like a big, heavy rock.

Tiffany stopped scooping and wrapped both her arms tightly around me and buried her head deeply into my left shoulder. This made it almost impossible for me to do anything to help anyone else.

"We're going to die!" Cindy screamed hysterically as we were tossed around like a bunch of rag dolls on a runaway roller coaster.

All hope quickly vanished when Charlie lost hold of his oar and it dropped into the swift current. Somberly I sighed as I watched it disappear from sight. Our nightmare only worsened when our boat slammed into a jagged rock. With one giant flip, our boat capsized, throwing us all into the freezing water.

Billy surfaced from the bottom of the river first, tightly holding his panicking sister in tow. Both struggled with all their might to reach the relative safety of the overturned boat while strong currents did their best to tear Cindy away from her brother.

Troubadour had Charlie's limp body pressed firmly against the side of the wrecked fishing boat. As strong as Troubadour was, it still took every ounce of his strength to keep the both of them from being ripped away and carried helplessly downstream.

Tiffany never surrendered her hold on me, even when we were submerged, making it easy to surface together. All those swimming lessons that my mother made me take every summer sure came in handy—I am an excellent swimmer now because of them. Gulping for air but trying not to swallow water, we finally made it over to the only life line we had—the capsized fishing boat.

One by one, we slowly pulled ourselves out of the frigid water onto the boat as Troubadour instructed us to do. Terrified, we held on for dear life while the raging waters swept us downstream. Now I have a better idea of the hopelessness that the passengers on the Titanic must have felt after hitting the iceberg. As we desperately clung to the boat, now shivering with our teeth chattering, I noticed that my friends' lips were all turning the color of Tiffany's eyes.

My thoughts flashed back to one of my mother's favorite sayings, which she used often, "If all your friends jumped off a high building, would that make it okay for you to follow?" Apparently I thought it did, considering my current situation. I wondered why I didn't try harder to stop my friends from casting off.

Totally at the mercy of the raging river, we twisted violently in every direction. It was like we were bronco-busting cowpokes riding the bucking waves.

Huddling together trying to get warm by our body heat, Tiffany broke the silence by asking "What were we thinking?"

Sobbing, Cindy answered, "I don't think we thought it through at all."

"No kidding!" I snapped irritably.

There was nothing more to be said so we sat silently clinging to the old, wooden boat while being swept down river with no hope of getting to land. We were fully reaping the consequences of our brainless decision to cross the river.

"If it wasn't for bad luck, we'd have no luck at all." I thought to myself, fully aware that the predicament we found ourselves in wasn't brought on by bad luck or good. It was simply the result of all the choices we had made up until now. Then, I reminded myself that big boys don't cry.

As bad as our circumstances seemed, they were about to get a lot worse. You see the boat in which we put our faith and full trust was now beginning to sink since it couldn't support our combined

weight in its damaged condition. The distress and utter fear expressed on my friends' faces said it all—We are going to drown!

Although we were all entertaining the same thought, Billy was the first one brave enough to say it. "It's really stupid to go to the Dark Hole when all we need to do is slip over the side and let go. We'll just drift off and go to sleep forever."

Cindy grabbed her brother's arm so hard she drew blood when her fingernails dug in. "No! You can't leave me!" she screamed.

"The way I see it, it's a no-brainer." Starting to cry, Charlie continued, "I've done nothing on this journey except slow you guys down." He positioned his limp legs with his hands preparing to slide his body into the freezing water. "Besides, aren't you guys tired of carrying this useless body around?"

"Wait a minute! What about your pact?" Troubadour shouted.

"What pact?" Charlie yelled.

"The 'one for all, and all for one' pact that you all made with each other." Troubadour answered.

"Oh, yeah," Billy said remembering.

"But we're sinking!" shouted Tiffany as the water reached up to our knees.

Panic-stricken, Cindy yelled, "Someone better do something and fast!"

We needed to lighten the load immediately to have any chance of staying afloat. I figured I'd have a better chance of surviving since I was the best swimmer. So with Tiffany still clinging tightly to my arm, I carefully stood up, getting ready to dive into the water and swim for the nearest bank.

Tiffany held on tighter and said, "No way, you can't! Remember, one for all and all for one." Then she kissed my cheek. It was the first time today that I felt warm!

Troubadour looked at us warmly and said, "I once read somewhere that there is no greater gift that someone can give than to lay down his life for a friend." With a tear trailing down his face, he said, "I will never understand why you guys try so hard to live, just to fight so hard to die."

Before we could stop him, Troubadour slid his body down the side of the boat into the water—and with one final thrust, pushed himself away from the safety of the boat. Troubadour fought the rough currents to stay afloat just long enough to shout, "It was my honor to have known you all. Always remember to follow your heart—for whatever the heart chooses, the mind will surely justify." Then the gentle giant disappeared into the murky, white-capped water without a trace.

Still stunned by the loss of our friend, we were shocked when our boat suddenly ran aground onto the stony bank on the opposite side of the river. After securing what was left of the boat, Billy lifted his sister onto dry ground. Tiffany slid down off the boat while Billy and I moved Charlie onto the river bank.

Cold and wet, we stood staring at each other trying to process what had just occurred. One by one, we each started to cry because we knew that our selfishness had cost us a good friend.

Cindy broke down first, then Tiffany, followed closely by Charlie.

I didn't break down until I said, "I can't believe my friend Troubadour is really gone." Then, I couldn't hold back the tears any longer.

"He was our friend, too…" sobbed Cindy.

"He certainly was a fascinating creature, wasn't he?" Billy murmured.

Leaning against a large boulder, Charlie said sadly, "I'm really going to miss the big guy."

Cindy cried, "Me, too!"

The longer I sat there the more heartsick I became, realizing that choices we make will greatly affect the people closest to us. It was our selfish decision that cost us the life of our close companion and dear friend.

The afternoon sun broke through the clouds bringing us some much needed relief and it helped to dry out our sopping clothes. We decided to rest awhile so we could get back some of our strength for the journey ahead. As we sat on the stony river bank huddled together, who should appear but that familiar old snake?

He slithered up and wrapped his body around a big rock, "What's up, guys? Been doing a little swimming today?" He flashed a sinister smile.

Trying to remain calm without any success, Tiffany demanded, "What do YOU want?"

"Well you, of course," Damien replied, pointing at all of us with a sweep of his tail.

Charlie said, "Don't you have anything better to do with your time?

Damien replied, "Nope. You have my full attention!" Then he continued, "By the way, why are you laying around being lazy? Shouldn't you be on your way?"

At this point, losing all patience from the day's events I screamed, "Why don't you slither back under the rock you came from? Can't you tell we've had a really, really bad day?"

Jokingly Damien asked, "Where's the big guy? Did you finally run Troubadour off like everyone else who happens to venture into your miserable, dreary little lives?"

Billy lowered his head and said, "You don't deserve an explanation—but Troubadour gave his life so we could live and continue on with our journey. Troubadour is gone because of our selfishness."

Damien snickered and said, "You won't need him anyway. All you need to do from here is follow the signs along the way to the Dark Hole."

Cindy timidly joined the conversation, "Which signs should we follow…the sun, the stars, maybe the moon?"

By now Damien was laughing so hard he almost fell off the rock. "Could you guys get any stupider if you tried? Let me try to explain this in a way even idiots could understand," he jeered. "Just follow the signs, you dummies!" using his tail, Damien pointed over to a sign painted in big, red letters with an arrow:

THIS WAY TO THE DARK HOLE →

81

He then uncoiled himself from the rock and disappeared into the tall grass. He stopped only long enough to flash a wicked grin then added, "Follow the signs—you're closer than you think."

One by one, we got to our feet. Our biggest concern now was what to do with Charlie since Troubadour was gone. After careful consideration, we decided to construct a more compact and lighter version of the original stretcher.

Billy and his sister searched for straight tree limbs that we could use for the main poles and braces. Tiffany and I gathered smaller leafy branches and reeds from a nearby bog, sending the local waterfowl flying. Charlie sat against the boulder and painstakingly braided the reed grasses into sturdy rope. In about an hour-and-a-half, our little project was completed.

With the leftover limbs, Billy and I constructed a small wooden cross and stuck it into the ground next to the boulder that Charlie was leaning on. The girls picked some beautiful purple violets and placed the flowers at the base of the rugged cross.

Not knowing what to say at Troubadour's memorial service, we decided to sing his little jingle, "Walking in love, walking in the light, every morning, noon, and night." By the end of the song there wasn't a dry eye among us.

It was now time to go. Charlie rolled over onto the new stretcher, crossing his fingers that it would hold his weight. As soon as Charlie was comfortable, Cindy and Billy grabbed one handle while Tiffany and I grabbed the other in unison.

"We did it, guys! Let's head out. On to the Dark Hole…!" I cheered as we half-heartedly started on our journey again. We were one big, happy family—minus our good friend, Troubadour.

CHAPTER 11
The Ultimate Protest

Not in a big hurry, we set a nice, slow pace for ourselves. Under different circumstances, we might have actually enjoyed our walk up the grassy path that snaked through the thick woodlands. We passed some large, moss-covered rocks bordering a small pond dotted with cattails. We stopped there to drink but were soon on our way—trying to ignore the hunger pangs which gnawed at our stomachs.

As we walked, the underbrush seemed to get thicker and thicker—so bad that we actually lost the trail at one point. It took us a long time to find it again, and once we did, the going was a lot rougher. We ducked branches and pushed aside the brush while trying hard not to dump Charlie, whose legs from the knees down were dragging the ground. It was his way of helping to lighten our load by not having them add weight to the stretcher.

We walked for what seemed like days, keeping close watch on the signs. The normal sounds that we'd grown accustomed to had mysteriously disappeared. Even the gentle breeze which followed us had vanished. It's as if everything in the woods had come to a screeching halt.

Then Cindy, with a dumbfounded look on her face, said, "What happened to all the animals?" Nothing moved around us, not even an insect. The silence was deafening. There was something definitely wrong with this place.

Looking around, Billy said, "Other than those two wild rabbits on the trail five miles back…you're right, Sis."

Tiffany observed, "And it's way too quiet…Listen!"

Charlie sat up and looked around. "I don't hear anything…"

"Exactly!" Tiffany whispered.

With his little sister tightening her grip on his arm, Billy mumbled, "Kind of spooky, isn't it?"

I tilted my head, listening intently and answered, "Sure is." With the first beads of nervous sweat starting to run down my back, I realized that the lump in my throat was making it hard to swallow.

I thought to myself, "Where did all the honey bees and colorful butterflies which fluttered among the wild flowers go… and the hundreds of starlings which darted from tree limb to tree limb, when did they disappear? Even the pesky mosquitoes were gone." The silence was heavy—you could have cut it with a knife!

After clearing my throat I managed to blurt out, "This is really weird! I wish Troubadour was here with us. He would have known what to do…" Man, did I miss the big guy!

Just then, the trail abruptly ended and we faced a large sign standing in front of us:

DARK HOLE - WELCOME TO YOUR DESTINY

Just moments after seeing the sign, a loud voice announced, "You have now entered the Dark Hole. Welcome to your destiny!" which made the place even more frightening because we couldn't tell where the voice was coming from.

Standing there, we all had the same weird feeling because the forest on the front side of that rustic, hand-lettered sign was a lush leafy green, beautiful and alive—all the way down to the sun-drenched moss which covered the ground at our feet. The forest on the back side of the welcome sign was the exact opposite!

Everything past the sign was dead, dying or decayed. This barren, godforsaken place was void of any living thing—except for us, of course. Still we entered that desolate piece of property at our own risk, driven by unseen forces pulling at us like a giant magnet.

My thoughts whirled about in my head as my knees knocked together in fear. Even the hair on the back of my neck came alive and was standing on end looking for a place to hide.

Wiping my sweat-drenched forehead, I heard Tiffany whisper to Cindy. "This place is haunted."

"Scary, too!" whimpered Cindy.

Charlie must have been reading my mind when out of nowhere he blurted out, "I sure wish Troubadour was here."

"I know what you mean...!"

Step by step, we journeyed further into this dreary place, so rightly named "The Dark Hole." None of us got more than an arms-length away from each other due to our mounting anxiety. As a result, we kept bumping into each other because one of us would sporadically stop to gawk at something. However, we soon grew accustomed to our new surroundings.

Scratching the side of his head in a disillusioned stare, Billy said, "Honestly, this isn't what I expected."

Sitting himself up Charlie added, "Me, either...."

Tiffany yawned and said, "If you ask me, this place could use one of those supreme makeovers."

"It's pretty drab around here, for sure," Cindy added.

"Not as drab as Bobby," joked Billy.

"Funny!" I snapped as I squatted down, pulled up a dead weed—roots and all, and lobbed it at Billy the Comedian's head. Unfortunately, instead of hitting Billy, it struck Tiffany on her right hip.

Wiping the dirty remains off of her once white Capri's, Tiffany voiced her disapproval by shouting, "Why don't you grow up, Bobby?"

Embarrassed by the mishap and feeling my face turn the shade of a vine-ripened tomato, I murmured, "Sorry" and gave Billy an unforgiving look. He just smirked and took his sister by the hand.

We walked on a few more yards and stopped abruptly. Looming in front of us was a huge gaping hole in the ground. Its opening was approximately ten feet across and thirty feet long. We inched closer for a better look.

Billy said, "Has anyone noticed how it's becoming hard to breathe around here?"

Struggling to take in a deep breath, Charlie gasped, "It's as if it's sucking the life right out of us."

The closer we got to the hole, the harder it was to get enough oxygen, and it was getting worse by the second. It was as if someone had placed a plastic bag over our heads and we were suffocating. Yet we continued to inch our way towards the cavernous Dark Hole.

After a painstaking effort, we edged just close enough to peer into the hole—keeping a safe distance away. What met our eyes was a vast expanse of nothingness. The depth was endless and it somehow seemed to be unrestricted by time and space.

I believe it was the first time I've ever seen the color black in action. The hole almost seemed alive. As we neared the edge it seemed to pull us closer, beckoning us to come in. We stood motionless almost hypnotized by the malevolent power before us.

Then something wonderful happened in the midst of all that ugliness. One drop of crystal clear water could be seen falling through the sky and disappearing quickly into the center of the Dark Hole. If it wasn't for the tiny prism of light that beamed out from the drop, we would have missed it altogether. What made it even more incredible was that the tiny drop, as it fell harmlessly into the hole, gave off the most beautiful fragrance of apple, cinnamon spice, and rosemary.

I looked at Cindy and asked, "Did you see that?"

Cindy replied, "Yes, I did, but what was it?"

Still awestruck, Tiffany exclaimed, "I will never, even if I live to be a hundred, see anything more beautiful!"

"It really smelled nice, too," commented Charlie as he eyeballed the hole, deciding his next move.

Charlie dragged himself over to the edge and peered into the darkness. As soon as Charlie's head hung over the opening, we heard that familiar hissing that always alerted us that Damien was near.

Sure enough, there he was in his self-centered splendor, rising up from the center of the Dark Hole. He rode a thick green mist that lifted him up like a genie on a magic carpet. The mist stunk horribly causing us all to gag and shrink back.

As the crafty old snake slithered from the mist onto solid ground, he started in with his constant complaining, "Well it's about time you pathetic losers got here. I guess you think I have nothing better to do with my time than accommodate you. Well, come on… Let's get this show on the road! Who's going to be first?"

We all stood silently near the edge of the opening of the Dark Hole. He slowly slithered behind Tiffany and nudged her from behind towards the hole. Damien hissed, "Well, how about you my bold, pretty one? Why don't you use that charm of yours and show them the way?"

Tiffany reached out to take my hand to help brace herself. Damien smiled and said, "That's the spirit, girl! You and Bobby can go together…sort of like Romeo and Juliet. It'll be wonderfully romantic!" He sighed and winked.

Damien then wrapped himself tightly around both Tiffany and me. He wound his muscular body about both our legs making it difficult to stay upright. Then, as his mouth twisted into a creepy, loathsome smile, Damien shouted, "Okay, you two, on the count of three….two…one…JUMP!"

I reached down with my hand and pinched the snake's mouth together to shut him up. "Hold it right there, Damien…Not so fast! Maybe I've reconsidered. I've been thinking a lot about my family lately and how this decision might hurt them."

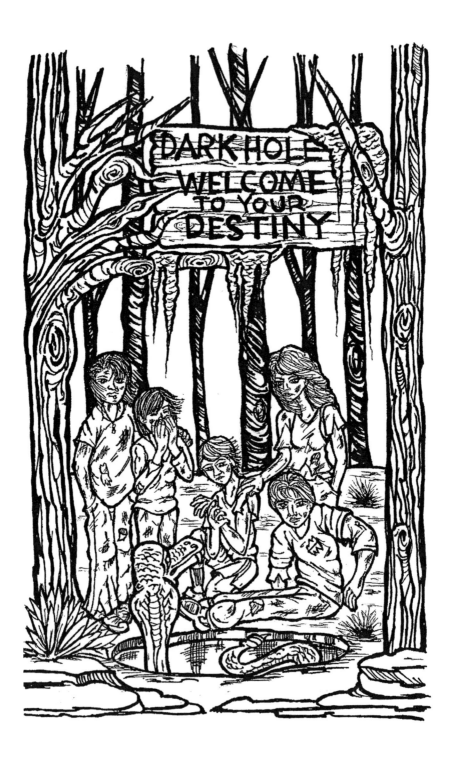

Damien snorted, "Your so-called family has never made time for you, Bobby. You are just an insignificant mistake that your parents have had to put up with for twelve long years. Bobby, they didn't even take time from their busy schedules to watch you play in the big game, did they? Oops, my bad! I forgot that you didn't have the opportunity to play in the big game, did you? You were too small or something…Nobody wanted you," smirked Damien.

The snake turned his attention to Tiffany and said, "And you, my pretty one. It must be really painful for you to know that no one on this big, giant planet cares about you. Remember when you were seven years old and your daddy dragged you across the carpet on your bedroom floor? You refused to let go of his ankle so that he could go on another business trip instead of staying home to play with his little spoiled brat…And remember how you cried yourself to sleep holding your little hand from where he stepped on it in his haste to catch his flight, never even looking back to see if you were hurt?"

With tears streaming down both of her cheeks, Tiffany asked Damien, "How do you know that?"

Slipping his tail gently around Tiffany's shoulders and looking deep into her eyes, "Who do you think held you all night long on that dark closet floor?" Inches from Tiffany's face Damien added, "Besides you and I both know your parents only keep you around because you are a tax write-off. The best thing you could do for everyone is to save the tax-payers some much needed money and finish what you started…just end it. End it now! You don't even have parents or a home to return to," Damien cruelly persisted.

Finally, releasing his grip on Tiffany and me, he slithered over to where Charlie was sitting. Damien demanded snidely, "How about you, cripple?"

Charlie continued to pick at the dead grass without responding to Damien's question.

"Let's face reality, Charlie. If you don't end the pain today, you won't be able to leave this place under your own power. Some poor sucker will have to carry your big sorry butt all the way home. FOR WHAT? So you can sit on the sidelines forever? Think about it! Who wants a kid in a wheelchair hanging around? NO ONE!" Damien rudely tapped his tail against Charlie's forehead and shouted, "Hello—is there anyone in there? I really don't think you get it, Charlie! So do yourself and everyone else a big favor and stop the suffering now."

Billy, hearing enough, grabbed Damien by the throat and made a tight fist with his other hand. "That's my friend you are humiliating and making fun of." He looked as if he was about to hit the snake upside the head.

I must admit, I don't believe I've ever seen Billy that angry since meeting him. It looked like Damien was about to get what he had coming to him—and get it good! Instead, and to my surprise, Billy took a deep breath and counted to ten. Then, releasing his tight grip on Damien's neck, Billy ordered, "Not another word! You got it, snake?"

With a renewed determination in her voice Tiffany said, "Yeah. Now what do you have to say, smart mouth?" She pointed her finger at Damien.

Damien coughed a couple of times, and then cleared his throat. He rose up on his tail as if ready to strike. Instead, he hissed then spit a venomous yellowish slime out from his fangs. The poison nearly hit Tiffany and me in the face. Angrily Damien responded. "Well what do you know, you losers found a little courage after all. Who would have thought that? You grew a new spine somewhere on your journey...how nice!"

Turning back to look at Charlie, Damien continued, "Not all of you, I guess." Covering his mouth with the end of his long tail, Damien began to laugh in Charlie's face. Angrily, Charlie took a swing at Damien as hard as he could, trying to punch the vicious snake right between his emerald eyes. Damien just laughed even harder when Charlie missed, taunting him with "Temper, temper, temper..."

Next, Damien turned his full attention back on Billy, even angrier than before. "How dare you put your hands on me, boy?

You're pretty brave for someone who still wets his bed, aren't you?" Snorting in disgust, Damien coiled his muscular body and sprang without warning at Billy. He wrapped himself tightly around Billy's body, pinning his arms to his side—rendering him helpless to do anything to defend himself. Damien let out an evil laugh and said, "What are you going to do now, bed wetter?"

Wincing in pain and gasping for air, Billy shouted, "I hate you!"

Damien wagged the end of his tail back and forth like a scolding finger, "It's not nice to hate."

Screaming at the top of her lungs Cindy shouted, "Leave my brother alone, you creep!" She grabbed Damien by the tail with both hands and proceeded to pull with all her might. She was trying desperately to get Damien to loosen his hold on her brother but with no success.

Damien just laughed and squeezed Billy even tighter. Billy's neck and face began to change from flesh color to a deep shade of reddish purple. Damien's hold was so tight by now, I thought Billy's head was going to explode right there in front of us. Suddenly, Damien loosened his grip and dropped Billy's limp body to the ground. Lowering himself down, he got eye-to-eye with Billy and said in a non-threatening voice, "Let's not fight, Billy. As a matter of fact, I think we could become good friends."

Crawling over to Billy and grabbing his legs, Charlie said, "Don't trust him, Billy!"

I kicked some dirt in the direction of Damien's head agreeing whole-heartedly with Charlie. "That's right! Damien can't be trusted, Billy!"

Smirking ever so slightly, Damien's whole manner changed. In almost a whisper he pleaded, "Come on, Billy. Let's sit down and reason together...I'm sure two minds are better than one. Maybe we can reach a solution to your dilemma together. Let's take a look at your circumstances and begin to weigh out your options." Smiling, he continued, "The choices you make will have grave consequences…And let's face it, you're not the brightest bulb in the box, are you."

Cindy grabbed her brother's hand and said, "Don't listen to him, Billy."

Damien casually slipped his busy tail around Cindy's waist and effortlessly lifted Billy's screaming sister three feet off the ground.

Simultaneously Tiffany and I yelled, "Put her down!"

Damien grinned and abruptly put the irate girl back on the ground several yards away from Billy. "I would greatly appreciate it if you would stop interrupting me. I am trying to have a conversation with your brother."

Turning back to Billy, Damien asks, "Now, where were we? Oh yeah, I remember…So let's focus only on the actions of your decisions, okay? If you decide to return home, what will you be returning to? We all know that your elevator doesn't go all the way to the top floor, does it? And because of that, you will have the honor of repeating the eighth grade all over again." Bobbing his head up and down Damien continued, "Billy, you remember how mean kids can be, don't you? Maybe if you're really lucky, they might put you in that special education class with all the other slow learners…" Damien paused only long enough to laugh, "Perhaps maybe all you need to do is try harder. I happen to know your mother is quite proud of her little flunky."

Damien looked at Charlie and said, "Did you know that Billy cries a lot at night when he thinks everyone is asleep? Or that Billy buries his head deep into his pillow to muffle his sobbing so his step dad won't come in and beat him for crying? Not that it's any of my business..."

"Good idea, why don't you start minding your own business?" I snapped.

"I sure wouldn't want to return home to that!" Damien hissed.

Hesitantly, Charlie looked to Billy for confirmation of what Damien had just said. Embarrassed, Billy didn't answer but instead sat on the ground and began to cry. Not fully understanding, Cindy went over to console her brother with one hand while taking a swing at Damien with the other yelling, "You're so mean!"

Damien said, "Whatever. It's obvious that there isn't a real back bone in the lot of you." He then crawled to the nearest tree and wrapped himself around the lowest hanging branch, content to observe us from his perch.

Tiffany said, "Troubadour was right, you guys. We need to see ourselves in a positive light and not give any thought to what others might think about us, including that nasty old snake."

Then I said, "Remember when Troubadour told us that if we would only shine the light of truth on the lies, it would free our minds to help us walk through the pain, instead of running from it. I sure wish Troubadour was still with us, don't you? I believe he would have been very proud of us today."

"I don't know about Troubadour, but I know I'm proud of us," Charlie said.

Billy bent down in front of Charlie, his newest friend and proudly said, "Charlie, it would be my honor to give you a lift home."

Charlie smiled and said, "Really? Thanks, man!"

Feeling an overwhelming sense of relief at the decision to forgo the conclusion of the Dark Hole, I stood at a distance and watched my new friends hugging and crying. I realized that I had a few tears in my eyes as well.

I decided it was time to lead my new friends back home and get them as far away as possible from this evil place. Without hesitation, I spun around and walked over to where Charlie and Billy were. Stretching out my sweaty, dirty hand, I proclaimed, "All for one, and one for all!"

With a look of contentment on Charlie's sun-beaten face, he put his blistered hand on top of mine and said, "Let's hear it for putting the needs of others before your own."

Placing his right hand on top of the pile Billy replied, "Let's hear it for setting and achieving personal goals" and he added, "Let's not forget the importance of teamwork!"

Tiffany's added her dainty hand to the stack, "And don't forget the value of positive self-worth and esteem. Yay!"

Finally, beating Billy for the top spot, I yelled, "One, two, three, break!"

I discovered that I was proud of the new confidence which I had found in myself. I gently took Tiffany's hand, gave her a shy kiss on the cheek, and happily said, "Let's go home." She smiled and squeezed my hand in approval.

CHAPTER 12
The Final Conflict

Realizing that Cindy hadn't placed her familiar hand on the stack, Billy turned around looking for his sister. As his gaze fell on the Dark Hole behind us, he let out a blood-curdling scream, "Cindy!"

What I saw next left me panic-stricken. We all froze like miniature statues completely unable to speak. Cindy was standing on the very edge of the Dark Hole's gaping mouth…so close that her toes were actually hanging over the edge. She was teetering back and forth on the brink of disaster as tears streamed down her cheeks.

We were frightened out of our minds for Cindy's safety. We realized she was fully committed to ending the pain that had haunted her young life for years—ending it once and for all.

As I stood holding my breath, I swear my heart must have skipped a couple of beats. I finally came out of my shock enough to shout, "Cindy, STOP!"

Damien clinging to a tree limb directly over her head, whispered in her ear all the things that would happen to her if she went home. He whispered that things would only get worse—that there would only be more pain waiting for her. He told her the voices would never leave her alone. With all the wickedness that old sinister snake could conjure up, he tried to convince Cindy to jump. Then he shouted, "DO IT! DO IT NOW! JUMP, CINDY!"

We headed towards Cindy but as we got closer to her, she held up her hand and warned, "If you come any closer, I swear I'll do it—I'll jump!"

So we stopped dead in our tracks and didn't move a muscle.

With her eyes tightly closed Cindy said, "Damien is right. If I return home, nothing will change. Billy, I love you but it hurts too much. I can't go home…I just can't!"

Without a moment of hesitation Billy, Tiffany and I dashed to where Cindy dangerously wavered on the edge of the Dark Hole. Suddenly a freaky windstorm appeared out of nowhere, sending strong gusts through the dead trees, snapping them like toothpicks. It stirred up dirt and debris from the parched ground, swirling it about like a miniature tornado. The grit blown into our eyes made it difficult to see.

Billy reached his sobbing sister's side first. Softly calling to her he begged, "Take my hand, Sis!"

Cindy simply lowered her head and said, "I'm sorry, I can't."

With tears trailing down his cheeks Billy promised, "Okay, Cindy…we won't go home. We'll just keep running."

"No!" Cindy shouted. "They will find us and send you away… and they'll make me go home."

Frustrated, Billy demanded, "Cindy, stop fooling around and take my hand. Now!"

Cindy sobbed and shook her head, "No, I can't…"

Wiping sand from my eyes and staying back at a safe distance, I calmly said, "Cindy come away from the hole. You won't have to go home. Come and stay at my house. We have plenty of room. I know my mother will be able to help us. She's a guidance counselor at our middle school. She knows who to contact and what to do. This never has to happen to you again, but you have to trust me. Step back from the hole, Cindy!"

Tiffany then stepped in front of Billy. Her voice was calm and confident as she spoke, "Hey, girl! You know us girls are going to have to stick together, don't you? So take my hand, sweetie…"

Cindy let out one last sigh as she wiped the remaining tears from her swollen, red eyes. With all the remaining faith she could gather, she reached out for the security of Tiffany's hand.

As Cindy and Tiffany's hands joined together, Damien immediately dropped from the tree limb directly onto Cindy's shoulders. The weight of the snake pulled Cindy over the edge. The two of them disappeared into the darkness of the hole but to our utterly joyous surprise, Tiffany still clung to Cindy's small wrist.

Unfortunately, the weight of Cindy's body started to pull Tiffany over the edge as well. Without hesitation, Billy and I fell to the ground each grabbing one of Tiffany's ankles. We braced ourselves as well as we could and hoped for the best.

Tiffany's voice began to crack as she cried out, "Please do something! I'm not going to be able to hold on to her much longer."

With her sweaty hand slipping from Tiffany's, Cindy cried out, "I'm falling! Help me, God..."

Just then the life line that Tiffany had with Cindy failed them both. Cindy's blood-curdling scream was the last thing we heard as Billy's little sister disappeared into the nothingness of the Black Hole.

With the sun setting behind us, we just lay there in a state of shock, staring at each other in utter disbelief. We were a helpless pile of defeated soldiers after a failed mission. We knew we would never see Cindy again, just like when we lost our friend Troubadour. What on earth would we tell Cindy's parents about what happened today?

Feeling sick to my stomach and about to throw up, I sat up hoping I could face the guilt I felt for the loss of both my friends. With tears trailing down my cheeks, I wondered how I could have let this happen—first, to my lovable, giant friend...and then to sweet, kind Cindy. Pounding my fist on the ground I shouted out, "Life can be so unfair!" wiping my puffy, red eyes I screamed loud enough to wake the dead, "Life Stinks!"

After what seemed like an eternity, though it was actually only seconds, Billy got to his feet and took about eight steps in the opposite direction of the Dark Hole, with Tiffany in hot pursuit and trying to apologize for not being strong enough to keep hold of Cindy's hand.

Pausing momentarily, he turned and grabbed Tiffany by both of her shoulders and planted the biggest kiss on her thin pink lips and said, "It's not your fault!" and he tenderly wiped the remaining tears from Tiffany's face.

Then without any emotion whatsoever, staring straight ahead in a trance-like state, Billy began walking towards the Dark Hole. He murmured to himself, "There's no reason for me to return home either, not without Cindy."

Once I realized what was taking place, I frantically screamed, "BILLY, PLEASE STOP!"

Billy continued walking towards the Dark Hole focused on accomplishing the task at hand, to join his sister at the bottom of the hole.

Jumping to my feet I knew I had to do something fast, but what? Something began stirring inside of me, a newly found courage that I've never experienced before. With no time to lose, I began sprinting towards Billy. With my head down I hit him right in the middle of his back, wrapping both my arms around him at the same time. I thought to myself it was a tackle any linebacker would have been proud of. We both tumbled to the ground and a trickle of blood appeared on both my elbows.

After rolling around on the ground for awhile I said, "Don't make me hurt you, Billy." We were both covered in dirt and Billy squirmed to get out of my grip. It was like wrestling an alligator! I was losing decisively due to the huge weight and size difference. Out of breath I gasped, "I could use some help over here!"

Just then Billy kicked me in the forehead, but I didn't release my hold on his leg. At least I had some help now—Tiffany was frantically trying to grab hold of his free leg. If it wasn't so serious, it might have been funny to see the two of us trying to hold Billy down so he couldn't complete his mission, surrendering his life to the Dark Hole.

Just then Billy broke free, leaving both of us behind laying face down in the dirt, like losers in a tug of war contest.

Then out of nowhere, like a guided missile with the Dark Hole as its target, our dear friend Troubadour shot past us, kicking up a cloud of dust. As he ran, his large lion body was undergoing a metamorphosis. He was transforming into a magnificent angelic being with enormous wings. His wings were as white as newly driven snow, lined with pure gold, and they glistened as brightly as sparkling diamonds.

We shielded our eyes from the overwhelming brightness of Troubadour's spectacular, glorified presence. As we watched in awe, the Troubadour we had known so well had morphed into a powerful angel, layer upon layer of muscles bulging, his reddish-brown hair flowing to his shoulders.

As soon as that angelic, winged creature disappeared down into the Dark Hole, lightning bolts and rolling thunder danced in harmony across the dismal sky. It was as if God himself showed up to visit.

After a couple minutes of ruckus, loud noises, and flying objects, Troubadour shot out of the Dark Hole like a launched rocket with Cindy tucked firmly away in his strong arms. Now victoriously above ground, Troubadour placed Cindy into her brother's arms.

This definitely was the perfect time for a group hug. We all took part, although hugging Troubadour was like hugging a thousand watt light bulb with bulging muscles. We didn't care, though, because we were all safe and sound and together again. I thought to myself that life couldn't get any better than this.

As quickly as Troubadour had re-entered our lives, we knew our reunion was going to be short-lived. Troubadour smiled affectionately and said, "It's been my honor to have spent this time with you on your journey of self-discovery. I knew you guys had it in you!"

"We can't thank you enough, Troubadour," Charlie said.

Feeling joy rise up in my heart as well, I added, "Yeah, thanks big guy!"

Finishing his thoughts, Troubadour continued by adding, "It's about making the right choices when no one else is watching. Even when the circumstances in your life have not turned out the way you had hoped."

Pulling her hair back into a ponytail Tiffany responded, "Sounds like you are talking about character, Troubadour."

"Exactly!" he said enthusiastically.

Gently tugging on Tiffany's golden ponytail, Troubadour winked and said, "Making the right choices in difficult times builds character."

Looking up at full moon that lit up the clear night sky, the angelic being apologized and then said, "But it is time for me to go…I must be about the Creator's business."

Troubadour tucked his enormous wings and gave each of us one last, gigantic hug. I was the last one in line for hugs. I waited until his arms were firmly around me, and then pleaded with him to stay with us and help us find our way home.

After taking a few steps away from me, Troubadour spread his wings majestically, turning he said, "You don't need me anymore…You have the Truth!"

Tiffany responded with a baffled look and said, "What truth, Troubadour?"

Billy chimed in, "Yeah. What truth?"

Troubadour said, "The truth about who you are and who I am. For you see, the truth will always set you free and whoever is free is free indeed. There's nothing you cannot accomplish through Him, the Creator." Troubadour pointed toward heaven with one finger, "With your heart in a right place, you can believe for anything."

Troubadour took a couple of steps back in our direction and placed one hand on Tiffany's shoulder and the other on Charlie's. "For whatever your heart chooses, the mind will surely justify."

Then our dear friend slowly turned his back to us and started to walk out of our lives again.

With tears welling up, Cindy ran to Troubadour and hugged his massive legs and said, "Thank you, Troubadour, for everything!" Then she ran back to her brother and took hold of his reassuring hand.

I yelled to him, "Hold it, Troubadour!" I ran to him before he could take another step. "Before you leave, can you answer one question for me?

Troubadour said, "Sure, if I can."

"My question, Troubadour, is this. When we were standing at the opening of the Dark Hole…Every so often one beautiful, crystal-clear drop of water would fall into the Dark Hole. Do you know what that was?"

Tiffany interrupted by adding, "Don't forget about the intoxicating aroma that came from each drop!"

Troubadour's wings came together and were raised high above him while he lowered his head at the same time in complete surrender and honor.

He said, "In heaven, there is a beautiful mountain that stretches beyond the clouds. And on this mountain is a throne that has an appearance of Jasper, like a Sardis stone and it sits on a sea of glass-like crystal which glows like a beautiful rainbow...And the One who sit on the throne, well…" A giant smile graced his face that almost made him glow. "And from the mountain proceeds continuous lightning, thunder and angelic voices are heard singing Holy, Holy, Holy."

Troubadour continued, "Every time a child such as you in a moment of helpless desperation chooses to end their life, thinking it to be their only solution—one tear from the Creator's holy cheek falls from the throne…it runs down the mountain, across the crystal sea at the speed of light… leaving the heavenly realms, gaining speed through eons of time and space. It then shoots down through the earth's atmosphere, landing in this precise place each time—One tear for every life."

I know we all must have had a blank stare on our bewildered, dust-covered faces by the look we received from Troubadour. As a matter of fact, we were so captivated by what Troubadour was telling us that none of us noticed that the once peaceful dark night skies had taken on a blood red appearance.

Even the moon was now crimson in color. Flashes of white lightning raced across the reddish-bronze sky with hurling jagged bolts of electricity. All of our hairs stood on end from the static in the air. Even the green mist permeating from the depths of the Dark Hole was arching brilliant blue sparks when coming in contact with the charged air particles.

It reminded me of a fourth of July celebration back home in Summerset. Right in the midst of all that cosmic confusion, that enormous angelic creature we once knew as Troubadour, the gentle giant, spread his magnificent wings until they completely surrounded the huddle we all stood in. He smiled once and said, "Now close your eyes, my young friends."

As soon as my eyelids closed tightly over my brown eyes, I fell into a deep sleep thinking about my newfound traveling companions and how I was going to miss smart-mouthed Billy and his feisty little sister Cindy, courageous Charlie, beautiful Tiffany and most of all my kind, loveable friend Troubadour, sent to us by God, our Creator.

Startled by a family of red-headed woodpeckers tapping out their morning message on nearby trees, I awoke huddled in a ball with my knees to my chest. Not knowing what to expect I slowly opened my blurry eyes, squinting from the brightness of the morning sun. As I sat under that willow tree, taking a couple minutes to fondly reflect on the wondrous events that transpired last night, I suddenly felt alone.

Shielding my eyes from the sun, I jumped to my feet realizing that somehow Troubadour had mysteriously transported me back to the exact place from which I started my journey. I mean it was the very spot beneath the tree branches that I had first met that evil, self-absorbed, reptile Damien.

After a few more moments of reflecting, I took one last look around and started the final stage of my journey—going back home. With a new perspective on who I am, and a newfound passion to get on with my life, I headed down the narrow trail.

As I walked under the perfect, cloudless sky I sang this jingle, "Walking in love and His light, every morning, noon and night."

I paused momentarily to wonder about my new friends. Smiling contentedly, I continued on my way knowing that with Troubadour in charge of their transportation, they were safe and completely prepared for their journey home.

An Important Note from the Author

Maybe you or someone you know has had thoughts of "ending it all." There are a few things you should know about suicide that I have learned through many years of counseling hurting teens and adults who were either considering suicide or had attempted it.

First, a single or random thought of "ending it all" does not mean someone is really "suicidal." Bobby Cooper soon recognized that his problems weren't very serious when compared to the pain that his companions had endured. Through his journey, he saw that his problems were not important enough to end his life. Instead, he chose to face them with courage and his new-found hope.

Second, most teens do not "suddenly" choose to take their life. Usually, there is not just one single moment or event that leads someone to want to "end it all forever." It is usually much more complicated than that. A life of depression, rejection, abuse, and other painful situations can create a feeling of hopelessness which can lead someone to choose suicide as an escape from their circmstances. There may be one event which is the "last straw" that moves a teen from being "at risk for suicide" to being "suicidal" but it didn't happen overnight. *Please note: even the "serious" events in the characters' lives were not good enough reasons to "end it all" as they eventually discovered. They had other options and they were not alone, two very important lessons that they learned on the way to the Dark Hole.*

Most importantly, if you believe you know of a family member or friend at risk for suicide and is showing one or more of the following signs: long periods of depression, anxiety or panic attacks, anger or rage, drastic mood changes, hopelessness and despair, reckless and hurtful behavior, loss of purpose, giving away treasured belongings, substance abuse, and the withdrawl from family, friends and organizations... it's not the time to look the other way--it's time to get involved and begin an open and honest dialogue before they cause harm to themselves.

If you feel inadequate to help them, please seek out help. I suggest contacting a school counselor, pastor or youth leader in your community, a trusted friend or family member...or if nothing else, you can contact a Crises Hotline, National Suicide Prevention Lifeline (800) 273-TALK (8255). There is also a wealth of information and support that can be found on the Internet.

If you would like to contact me, you may do so by the following means:

E-mail: rraver@ronaldraver.com
Please type "In Search of the Dark Hole" in the subject line.

Please visit my website at http://www.ronaldraver.com

Note: I am available to speak to churches, youth groups, and school assemblies. Please tell your leaders...

Stay tuned for my next book which is coming soon:

Bobby and Troubadour Reunite: In Silent Screams

Printed in the United States
217669BV00002B/1/P